The Perfect Illusion

WINTER RENSHAW

1

3

BOOKS BY WINTER RENSHAW

The Never Series

Never Kiss a Stranger

Never Is a Promise

Never Say Never

Bitter Rivals: a novella

The Arrogant Series

Arrogant Bastard

Arrogant Master

Arrogant Playboy

The Rixton Falls Series

Royal

Bachelor

Filthy

The Amato Brothers Series

Heartless

Reckless

Priceless (a Rixton Falls crossover)

Standalones

Dark Paradise

Vegas Baby

Cold Hearted

It's only pretend...

And it's only three months.

I'm in the midst of scrawling "I QUIT!" onto his fancy cardstock letterhead when my boss corners me. He needs a favor, he says. And then he asks how well I can act …

Hudson Rutherford needs a fiancée.

With his old-moneyed parents forcing him to marry some bratty hotel heiress and his hedonistic, playboy lifestyle at stake, the only way to get them to back off is to make them think he's truly, madly, deeply in love … with me—his third personal assistant this year.

But I can hardly stand working for him as it is.

Hudson is crazy hot and well-aware. He's arrogant, spoiled, and silver-spooned. He checks me out when he thinks I'm not looking, and his life is a revolving door of beautiful women. Plus, he can't even pronounce my name correctly—how's he going to convince his family he's in love with me?!

I'm seconds from giving him a resounding "no" when he flashes his signature dimpled smirk and gives me a number that happens to contain a whole mess of zeroes …

On second thought, I think I can swallow my pride.

But, *oh baby*, there's one thing I haven't told him, one teensy-tiny thing that could make this just a hair complicated …

Here's hoping this entire thing doesn't explode in our faces.

Epigraph

They say time heals all wounds, and the scars you left are fading. I trace them with my fingers and try to make myself feel even a fraction of what I did when you left. It may not have been love but it was the most I've ever felt. — S. Stepp

Chapter One

Mari

Dear Mr. Rutherford,

I humbly request for you to accept this as my two weeks' notice. As of Friday, May 26th, I will be stepping down from my position as your personal assistant. I'll do my best to ensure this is a smooth transition for the company.

Sincerely,

Maribel Collins

I press my pen into his thick cardstock, scratching out my neatly written resignation before crumpling the paper in my hand and pushing it to the corner of my desk. It's too nice, and Hudson Rutherford does *not* deserve nice.

It's half past seven, which means I have thirty minutes to come up with something better than this—something that's going to leave a lasting impression.

I'm his third personal assistant this year and

it's only May. There's a reason no one can tolerate working for him longer than a month or two, and someone ought to point this out to him.

Might as well be me.

Clearing my throat, I try again.

Hudson,

You're rude and inconsiderate, and I no longer wish to work for you. You think the world revolves around you. Your excessive wealth disgusts me, as does your secret Rolodex of women's phone numbers that you keep hidden in your third desk drawer on the left. Your good looks are overshadowed by your vanity and arrogance, and your kindness, I'm convinced, is non-existent. You treat your employees like indentured servants, and you're the most hypocritical asshole I've ever met.

I work sixty hour weeks for you without so much as a thank you, a raise, or a glowing performance review. I'm tired of running your menial errands, and I didn't spend four years in college to make photocopies and coffee.

I didn't sign up for this.

You lied to me.

With zero fondness and absolutely no gratitude,

Mari

Sighing, I crumple this one too. I think my message got lost amongst all the spiteful word vomit, and the last thing I want to do is come across as trite.

Fed up is what I am.

Tired.

Underutilized, underpaid, and overworked.

But not trite.

I toss the wrinkled paper in the waste basket and grab one last sheet of letterhead. Ditching the formalities, I decide to go a more direct route. My mother once told me it's not in what you say, it's in what you don't say. And my father always says actions speak louder than words. Maybe I've been overthinking this whole resignation letter? With my pen firmly gripped, I scrawl my final version.

Hudson,

I QUIT.

Mari

It's perfect.

Smirking, I admire my work, fold it into thirds, then slide it into a cream-colored envelope with Rutherford Architectural's logo in the upper left corner. Licking the seal and scribbling his name on the front, I stick it on top of a pile of mail I plan to hand to him the second he arrives. I'll give him a moment to read it, and while he's doing so, I'll pack up my things and make a beeline for the elevator before he has a chance to stop me.

"Mary." I glance up from my workstation to see Hudson strolling into work in his signature navy suit and skinny black tie. He's early today.

"It's Mari," I correct him for the millionth time, inhaling his cedar and moss cologne. It's the only thing I've come to like about this man. "Rhymes with *sorry*—remember?"

His eyes narrow in my direction, and as he angles toward me, I see his right hand lifted to his ear. He's on the phone.

Hudson says nothing, only gathers the mail from the corner of my desk and strides down the hall toward the enormous glass-walled office that tends to make my stomach twist every time I have to walk in that direction.

This entire office space was his design. Glass walls. Zero privacy. Everything is clean-lined and modern. Chestnut-colored leather seating, white walls, reclaimed wood, and custom mid-century modern lighting installations are working in tandem here to create a space buzzing with creative inspiration, and all decorative accessories have to be approved by the head honcho himself. I tried to bring in a gray ceramic planter last month for my dendrobium orchids, and Hudson said it was too drab and industrialist. He claimed it would fuck with his energy—and he uses words like "fuck" and "energy" because he thinks he's some kind of renaissance boss.

My heart's pounding crazy fast, and I'm stuck trying to determine if I should bolt now or wait. Hudson usually checks his mail first thing in the morning, but for all I know, he's still on his phone call.

Drumming my fingers against my glass desktop, my feet remain firmly planted on the wood floor, though they may as well be frozen solid. The second my phone rings, it sends my heart leaping into my throat. I'm not afraid of him—I just hate drama. And I have a feeling Hudson's going to try to make this into a big thing.

"Yes?" I answer, my eyes scanning the caller ID. Hudson's extension flashes across the screen.

He exhales.

Oh, god.

He read it.

And now, the moment of truth.

"Mary, what is this?" he asks.

"What is ... *what*, sir?" I ask. And that's another thing—what kind of twenty-nine-year-old architect demands to be called "sir?"

"This invitation to the Brown-Hauer Gala? RSVPs were due two weeks ago. Call and find out if it's not too late," he says, his voice monotone. The tear of paper fills the background. He's quiet.

"I thought you said you didn't want to go?" I ask. I'm not sure why I'm phrasing this as a question because he *did* say he didn't want to go. As a matter of fact, I know I have it in an email ...

"I said that?" he asks, a sardonic chuckle in his question.

"Yes."

"I don't remember saying that." He exhales. "I never would've said that. Not to the Brown-Hauer. That gala hosts the who's who in the architectural world, are you fucking kidding me?"

His voice raises slightly, and my breath seizes. I should just hang up and get the hell out of here.

"Mary," he says.

"Mari," I correct. "*Rhymes with sorry.*"

In case he didn't hear me two minutes ago ...

"Can you come back here for a second?" he asks, his voice as stiff as his winning personality. "There's something we need to discuss. Immediately."

Anxiety forces my jaw into a tensed state. I shouldn't let this asshole get to me, and I know that, but he's literally the boss from hell. People like him are the reason happy hour was created.

At least he won't be my boss for much

longer.

I'm almost positive he's read my note and he's calling me back to try and talk me out of it, but I refuse.

My stomach churns, and I think I'm going to be sick—but not because I'm nervous.

Not because he scares me.

But because I'm pregnant.

And morning sickness is one hell of a bitch.

"I need a minute," I say, reaching for the bottle of room temperature water in front of me, though the sight of it intensifies my nausea. I meant to stop for saltines and ginger ale on the way here this morning, but I spaced off because I was too preoccupied with second-guessing my decision to quit my job so abruptly with single motherhood on the horizon.

"*You* may have a minute to spare, but *I* don't," he says. "Whatever it is, I'm sure it can wait. My office. Now."

Hudson hangs up before I have a chance to protest, and before I can stop myself, I'm marching back to his office like Darth Vader on a mission, heavy breathing and all.

I'm doing this.

I'm standing my ground.

I'm quitting.

And I'm walking out of here with my head held high.

Normally I'd knock three times on his door and wait for him to tell me to enter, but seeing how all the walls here are made out of crystal-clear glass, he's looking directly at me. And I'm seconds from quitting, so I don't see the need.

Rushing into his office, I place my hands on my hips and plant myself in the doorway. Hudson reclines in his chair, his hands resting behind his neck as his full lips hold an amused little smirk that perfectly contradicts the snarky tone he took with me a few moments ago.

Everything about this man is a walking contradiction, and it drives me crazy.

"What's with the attitude, Mary?" he asks, eyes scanning me from head to toe and back. "It's Friday. Lighten up."

I glance at his desk where my letter rests on top of the mail pile.

He hasn't opened it yet …

"What did you need?" I ask, but only because I'm curious. I don't actually intend to do a damn thing for this smug asshole from this moment on.

"Did you get my email this morning?" he asks.

Ah, yes. The infamous pre-work emails he sends from his treadmill at five in the morning. Not going to miss those.

My brows meet. "I haven't had a chance to check it yet."

"I'm going to need you to pick up my dry cleaning at ten. Drop everything off at my place afterwards, then stop by Palmetto's Deli to grab me a number four with no mustard. And make sure you check it before you leave. Last time you didn't, and you know how much I despise soggy bread. Oh. And after lunch, I need you to call the Brown-Hauer foundation and get me on the list for their gala. Email me as soon as you're finished so I know you didn't forget …"

He's rambling on, but I tune him out. My fists clench at my sides, and my vision darkens. He doesn't need to qualify his requests with insults.

This ...

This is why I hate this man.

This is why I have to quit. Immediately.

He's a micromanaging control freak.

I don't care what he says, I refuse to let him talk me out of this.

I came to Manhattan with a gleam in my eye, my little Nebraskan heart filled with optimism and hope. I wanted to be successful. I wanted to be someone.

Little did I know, nobody in New York cares if you graduated at the top of your class at some private college north of the Bible belt that no one's ever heard of. All that matters out here is who you know. And if you don't know anyone? Then you have one of two options: screw your way to the top, or work your ass off and hope that someone throws you a bone.

I had every intention of doing this with integrity, but clearly accepting a position at Rutherford Architectural was a bad move in the wrong direction.

So much for building up a respectable curriculum vitae.

"Mary, are you listening?" he asks, leaning forward in his chair, his elbows resting on his glass desk. Behind him is an expansive view of downtown Manhattan flanked by floor-to-ceiling bookshelves filled with every architectural college text, magazine, and coffee table book known to man. If there's one other positive thing I could say about Hudson Rutherford—besides the fact that he smells like money and oozes obnoxious charm that apparently no one but me can see through—it's that he's passionate about architecture. The man lives, sleeps, and breathes design.

If I wasn't so busy hating Hudson, I'd probably find his intense passion kind of sexy ...

"No," I say.

"Excuse me?" he scoffs, smoothing his thin black tie down his muscled chest before straightening his shoulders.

"When you speak to me like that," I say, holding my head high, "it makes me want to tune you out. I can't help it. It's an automatic reaction."

His jaw clenches, but his eyes glint, and I wonder if he's ever had an assistant speak up before.

Doubtful.

"Am I supposed to speak to you like you're on my level? Like we're equals?" he asks, chuffing. "Mary, I'm your boss. Your *superior*."

"Which is exactly why you should talk to me with a little more respect. It's called being professional." My lips are tight and numb. I can't believe I'm saying this … "I make your coffee. I field your calls. I grab your lunch. I do anything and everything you ask because let's face it, I'm the idiot who signed up for this job, but you treat me like your whipping post. If you forget something, it's always my fault. If *someone else* forgets something, it's always somehow my fault. If you're having a bad day, it's my fault. If I only work sixty hours instead of my scheduled forty, you make me feel like a slacker. If I ask for a day off, nine times out of ten, I'm told 'no.' It's exhausting working for you, Hudson. It's only been two months, and I can't do it anymore."

"So what are you saying?" he asks. I try to get a read on his expressionless face, but it's impossible. He's a man who holds his cards close to his chest at all times. I'm not sure whether he's panicked, relieved, or something else entirely.

Pointing to the letter on the top of his mail pile, I say, "I quit."

I turn on my heels and show myself out of his office, hurrying to get the hell out of the place I've come to call the Pristine Palace for the last two months.

"Wait," he calls after me as I head for my desk to gather my things. I glance behind me, only to see him standing in his glass doorway. "I'd like to make you an offer before you go."

Ha. Just as I expected.

I smirk, rolling my eyes as I keep walking. "No thanks."

"Mary." There's a deep husk in his voice, but I continue strutting away, my heels clicking on the reclaimed wood floor.

When I reach my desk, I grab my bag from the bottom drawer and toss a few personal items inside: my hand cream, lip balm, a tiny bag of emergency chocolate, and my back up water bottle. I'd toss some company pens in there too because they're fancy as hell, but I prefer never to so much as glance at the Rutherford Architecture logo ever again. Before I forget, I slide the elevator key to his penthouse apartment off my keyring and slap it on the desktop.

"Fine." The sudden, close proximity of

Hudson's voice jumpstarts my heart. I glance up to see him standing before me, his smooth hands splayed across my desk and his back arched. His sapphire blue eyes meet mine, refusing to let them go. "You can quit. Be my fucking guest. I'll have you replaced by tomorrow afternoon."

I offer a faux smile. "Glad everything's going to work out for you."

I fling my bag over my shoulder and stand tall, eyes grazing past his shoulder toward the elevator bay where the doors part and Hannah from Accounting steps off. Our eyes meet, and she gives me what is clearly her "Oh, shit ..." face.

It's a shame I won't be sticking around long enough to tell her everything's fine. Everything's abso-fucking-lutely fine.

"Goodbye, Hudson. And best of luck in finding a suitable replacement. I'm sorry I couldn't be what you needed." I move out from behind my desk and give him a sarcastic smirk, only I'm not prepared when he slips his hand around my wrist and guides me closer to him. "What the hell are you doing?"

I yank my hand from his, clutching it against my chest, fingers balled into a tight fist.

"One last thing before you go …" he says, his eyes softening just enough that I almost believe he's being sincere for the first time since I've known him.

Trying not to laugh too loud, I shake my head. "No."

"Hear me out," he says.

"Why should I?"

"Because I'll make it worth your while."

Rolling my eyes, I suck in a deep breath, mulling over the extent of my curiosity. What could he possibly need from me, a disgruntled employee in the midst of storming out of his office?

My stomach gurgles and another wave of morning sickness evolves into an impressive hot flash. A sheen of sweat forms across my forehead. I think I'm going to be sick, and if he doesn't get the hell out of my way, I'm about to be sick all over his immaculate Prada suit.

The wave passes, dissipating into nothing, and I pull in a clean breath of the hospital-grade air Hudson insists on piping through the office vents because it helps "keep his energy clean."

"I'm sorry," I say, "but there isn't anything

you could say or do at this point that would convince me to work another day next to you. I won't be doing you any favors, Hudson. You disgust me."

Oh, god. Here comes another round of word vomit, rising up my chest with unstoppable force.

"You walk around like you're better than everyone," I add. "You're self-centered. And arrogant. And cold. And inconsiderate. And rude. And you're delusional if you think you're going to get me to stick around, so, goodbye."

The corner of his mouth smirks, revealing a half-second flash of a dimple that sends an inconvenient and unexpected weakness to my knees. I hate how distracting and disarming his good looks are.

"Calm down, Mary." His voice is low, and when he leans in close, I find myself inhaling—and enjoying—the warm, musky scent radiating off his skin. "I know I'm a pain in the ass to work for. Well aware."

"Then why don't you try to change that?"

"Why should I? There's an entire city full of girls just like you begging to work here. Why should I have to change who I am to accommodate them? Besides, there's a whole world of assholes just like me—no, worse than me—waiting on the outside. If my employees can't handle me, they're sure as hell not going to be able to handle the next guy. The way I see it, I'm doing you all a favor. I'm prepping you for the real world."

"I refuse to believe bosses like you are the norm."

"Then you're extremely naïve." He huffs, his indigo-blue eyes lifting to the ceiling then back to me. "Anyway, three million dollars."

"Three million dollars—*what?*" I squint at him, not sure where he's going with this.

"If you agree to help me out, I'll give you three million dollars. Cash. And then you'll never have to work with this insufferable asshole ever again."

He's got to be joking.

"Aside from the fact that you've officially lost it, I'm not sticking around, not here. Not as your personal assistant. I'm better than this."

"I'm not asking you to be my personal assistant."

"Okay, whatever it is, I'm not interested. I

have a degree in business analytics and international marketing with a minor in finance." My arms tighten across my chest. I'm not interested in his bait money or whatever the hell kind of stunt he's attempting to pull. "I know my worth, and I know when a job isn't worth it."

"So you understand that three million dollars is a pretty generous amount of money, yes? Since you, uh, minored in finance and you know all about … worth?" He's trying to fight a smile, like he's not taking me seriously.

"Can you not?" I lift my hand to my right hip.

"Not what?"

"Can you not be so patronizing? It never ends with you."

"I'll work on it," he says. "*If* you stick around."

"No need," I remind him. "I'm not."

"Swallow your pride and agree to help me," he says. "You won't regret it."

"*No*," I say with as much conviction as I can drum up. A wave of nausea rolls over me once more, a silent reminder that it's not about me anymore. "Whatever it is ... no."

About a month ago, after a sexually debilitating dry spell no twenty-five-year-old should ever have to endure, I downloaded one of those stupid dating apps that everyone knows is really only used for hooking up, and I found myself the perfect one-night stand.

I thought I was smart about it. I'm on the pill. He used a condom. All precautionary measures were taken.

He was Ivy League educated, or so he claimed, and he had one of those rich people names, Hollis. His photos were all Nantucket and sailboats and he quoted F. Scott Fitzgerald in his bio. When we met, Hollis was friendly and well-mannered, well-groomed and clean cut. With disarming honey brown eyes and thick, sandy brown hair, he was everything he had shown himself to be. And the night was satisfying enough if not a little boring. But it filled the void and accomplished the mission, and we both went on our ways.

But a few days ago, I happened to pop open my birth control pack and realized I was three days past my week of sugar pills with no sign of Aunt Flo. An hour later, I'd purchased a variety of highly sensitive pregnancy tests from the local Duane

Reade, never believing in a million years I'd find myself face-to-face with a myriad of pale blue plus signs and pink happy faces.

That's the day the bottom dropped out.

Hollis was the first person I called—it only seemed right since he was the father. But his number was conveniently no longer in service. I had no way of getting a hold of him and no way of knowing what his last name was. I even spent hours trying to find him again on the dating app, but it was as if he'd just disappeared into thin air.

So now it's just us …

Me and this tiny little life I'm now fully responsible for—on my own.

This weekend I'll pack up my place, rent a moving truck with whatever credit remains on my MasterCard, and hightail it back to Nebraska. I can't afford to raise a baby in this city, at least not by myself. And now that I don't have a job, I can't afford the rent on my shoebox studio anyway.

"You're a fool." Hudson watches me sling my purse over my shoulder, and then he eyes the elevator bay in the distance. "With this money, the right investments, and a little time, you could be an extremely wealthy woman. Now you're going to spend the rest of your life working for assholes exactly like me because you were too proud to say yes to this one little favor."

"You're planting doubt in my head," I say. "You're trying to manipulate me. I see through you, Hudson. Always have. You're nothing more than a self-serving asshole. You couldn't shut it off if you tried."

"You're right. Me and every other man in this city." His soft, strong hands slip into his pants pockets and he exhales like a man who shamelessly owns his behavior and makes no apologies. "Anyway, aren't you curious? Don't you want to know what I want from you?"

"Not really." My lips bunch in one corner. "You pay me forty grand a year here, which isn't really a livable wage in this city, I might add. And you work me to the bone. I shudder to think of how much work three million dollars would entail."

"Can you act, Mary?" he asks, ignoring my refusal.

"That's random."

"It's not random at all. It's pretty straightforward. Stop wasting my time and answer it."

"I was in drama club in high school," I say, smoothing my hair from my face and pulling my shoulders back like a proud drama nerd. "And for a couple years in college. I've done community theatre as well."

Hudson *smiles*.

I've never seen him full-on smile like this.

"Perfect." His blue eyes crinkle at the corner. "I have to have you, Mary. You're hired."

My jaw hangs. "I'm … *what*? I didn't say … I don't want … no."

Hudson wraps his hand around my wrist, pulling me just outside the front doors of the office and out of earshot of the rest of his staff.

"Listen," he says, voice low. He tightens the space between us. "I'm sure you're wondering what the fuck I'm about to propose, and rightfully so. But believe me when I tell you it's going to change your life. And mine — because I'm a self-serving bastard and we both know that. But it'll be the easiest three million you'll ever make in your life, and when it's all said and done, you'll never have to see me — or work for anyone like me — ever again. It's win-win, Mary. And you'd be a damn fool to walk away."

I inhale, harboring a breath before letting it

go. When our eyes meet, I silently chide myself for remotely considering making a deal with this devil.

Sure, he's impossibly handsome with his chiseled jaw, dimpled smirk, coffee-colored hair, steel blue eyes, runner's build, designer wardrobe, and genius IQ—not that I've taken inventory of his *assets* before … but none of that is enough to overpower the ugliness that resides beneath his perfect, polished façade.

Without saying a word, I turn on my heel and press the call button on the nearest elevator.

"What are you doing?" he asks, voice rushed.

The doors part, and I step on, flashing a smirk and shrugging my shoulders. "Being a damn fool."

Chapter Two

Hudson

The overpowering scent of curry and fried takeout smacks me in the face when I enter her building, and the stairway to the third floor is poorly lit and narrow—clearly not up to code. I check the email on my phone once more, ensuring I have the right place, and then I turn the corner at the top of the stairs.

My gaze lands on the crooked number five at the end of the hall, and I straighten the knot of my tie before clearing my throat and proceeding.

This woman hates me—literally hates me—and I'm about to ask her an enormous favor. But it's precisely the reason she's perfect for this.

Three knocks on her door a moment later fail to elicit an answer, so I try again. And again. This building is noisy and busy, but I swear I hear someone shuffling around on the other side of the door.

She stormed out of my office earlier this morning, and while the question has been lingering on the tip of my tongue for hours now and I'm not accustomed to taking "no" for an answer, I figured I should give her some time and space before approaching her again.

"I know you're in there. Open up," I call through the door, knocking yet again. "Seriously, I don't have all day, I — "

The door swings open and my future fiancée stands on the other side, a hand on one curved hip and her sultry, hooded blue eyes glaring in my direction.

"What are you doing here?" she asks with the raspy, Scarlett Johansson voice that's driven me wild since the day she waltzed into my office in a tight little pencil skirt and an almost-transparent white button-down.

Peering over her shoulder, I glance into what is clearly a studio apartment approximately the size of my walk in closet. Furnished with flea market finds and a garish color scheme that makes zero sense, it immediately makes my skin crawl, but I shake it off because I didn't come here to critique the way she designs her living space. Besides, she's going to be living with me soon enough, and this place will become all but a distant memory.

"We weren't able to finish our conversation earlier." I straighten my shoulders, peering down. She's dressed in tight black leggings and a pink t-shirt that stops just beneath her navel, leaving her midriff slightly exposed. My cock pulses against my slacks. "May I come in?"

Her nose wrinkles, but her Midwestern manners won't allow her to slam the door in my face. Sighing, she steps back, letting the door open a little wider, and step inside.

"Thank you, Mari," I say.

"Wait. So you *do* know my name."

"Of course I know your name. I'm not an imbecile."

"So why'd you always—"

"—I have my reasons." I offer a haughty smirk. "It creates interpersonal distance, which I find is ideal for workplace relationships. An assistant should never get too close to her employer. Or too comfortable. I also wanted to test your patience, see how well you worked under frustrating circumstances."

She lets out a sarcastic huff. "Mission accomplished, Hudson. Bravo. Well done."

I glance at the stove several steps behind her, where she appears to be making ramen.

"Are you hungry, Mari?" I ask.

The timer beeps, and she grabs a nearby bowl, dumping the boiling water and soggy noodles in one fluid movement. It lands with a wet plop.

"Yeah," she says, eyes squinting. "But I've kind of got a handle on that right now, so please. Say what you came here to say because I'm about to eat my dinner, catch up on some *Game of Thrones*, and pretend like today wasn't one of the most annoying days of my life."

Mari takes a seat at a makeshift island barely big enough to accommodate two small bar stools and wraps her noodles around her fork, blowing on them with her full, cherry lips before taking a bite.

I chuckle. "All right. Fine. I came here because I want you to marry me."

She begins to cough, her hands covering her mouth, and I go to her, placing my hand on the small of her back.

"You okay?" I ask.

She nods, trying to catch her breath. Reaching for a napkin, she wipes her mouth before crushing it in her hand.

"Don't flatter yourself," she finally responds. "I would never marry you."

"Here's the deal," I say. "We're approaching summer, which, in the Rutherford family, means wedding season and a four-week mandatory stay at the family estate in Montauk. I'm turning thirty next month, and my parents have a sort of agreement with the Sheffield family that if I'm not married by thirty, I'll be promised to their daughter, Audrina. Our mothers have literally been counting down the days since we were babies, chomping at the bit to plan the wedding of the century."

"No one can force you to marry someone you don't want to marry."

"Ah, maybe that's so for most, Mari. But not in my family. My parents have ways," I say. "They won't hesitate to make my life ... *difficult* ... if I don't adhere."

"So you want them to think you're already engaged? What happens when the jig is up and you're still thirty and unmarried?"

"This is why I'm offering you three million

dollars," I say. "For the next three months, through wedding season and the family month at Montauk, I want you to play the part of my dutiful, head-over-heels in love fiancée. You must be convincing—*we* must be convincing. At the end of the three months, you'll receive half of your payment."

She lifts a brow. "Okay, so how would I earn the rest?"

"By marrying me." I clear my throat. "On paper."

Her expression falls. Clearly the idea holds zero appeal.

"Until Audrina finds some other poor schmuck to shackle herself to, I need you to be my wife. *Legal* wife. You don't have to live with me after this summer. In fact, you don't have to see me ever again. You simply have to be the name on the marriage certificate that assures my parents that I'm one hundred percent off the market."

"What if she takes years to find someone? What if she never finds someone? I'm just supposed to put my life on hold?"

"Kind of," I say with a gentle wince. "I know it's not ideal, but that's where the other half of your payment comes into play. In the meantime, you'll be free to date as you please. You'll be free to fall in love. You just won't be free to legally marry until we're able to quietly dissolve our arrangement."

"What about holidays? Won't your family wonder where I am at Christmas?"

"My parents go to Aspen for Christmas. I hate skiing, so I never join them. Our month at Montauk each summer is about the extent of our family togetherness. I'd be happy to make excuses for you in the coming years. Anyway, I don't anticipate Audrina will be on the market very long. She's been holding off for me, but rumor has it she's got a short list of waiting suitors in her back pocket, and she's got baby fever something fierce."

She pushes her half-eaten bowl of ramen away, resting her head in her hands and staring blankly ahead as if she might actually be contemplating this.

"What? What are you thinking?" I ask.

Her brows lift. "That this entire thing sounds insane. And that *you're* insane."

"Maybe it is. And maybe I am. But I know it could work."

She turns to me, her eyes holding mine.

"Why me, though? I can't stand you and you're well aware."

"That's exactly why it has to be you."

"You can't tell me that out of the assortment of women I've seen waltzing in and out of your life the last two months, not one of them would be jumping at the chance to help you with this."

"You're right. They would be. But then they'd want something more, and quite frankly, I have nothing more to give than my last name and a comfortable lifestyle," I say, checking my wristwatch. "You, Mari … you wouldn't want more from me, and that's exactly why you're the only one I trust."

"I don't know how I could convince anyone I'm in love with someone who gets under my skin the way you do, Hudson."

"You said you could act." I lift a brow.

"I … yeah … I guess? But can you?"

Stepping toward her, I take her by the wrist and guide her off the bar stool, pulling her body against mine, meeting her curious gaze with my own sultry version. Cupping her soft cheek in my right hand and letting my fingers graze the nape of her neck, I lift her mouth, holding mine inches from hers.

She breathes me in, her stare unblinking. My left hand circles her waist, feeling it cave with my touch.

"I've never told you this before ... but the day I met you, I knew there was something special about you. And something tells me you're about to become the best thing that's ever happened to me," I say, my words slow and gentle as our eyes lock. "I want to spend the rest of my life with you, until we're old and gray. We might drive each other crazy, our path may be a bit bumpy at times, but we're going to love every minute of it. Marry me, Maribel Collins. Be my wife. I don't want anyone but you."

Stillness lingers between us, and then she releases a shuddering breath before blinking. Peeling herself from me, she tucks her thick blonde hair behind her ears before resting her hands on her hips.

"That was ..." Mari leaves her thought unfinished as she moves a few paces back. "That was ... *cheesy*. But passable." Her lips pull into an bitten grin as she recovers her composure. "You're good at that." Glancing up at me, her expression dissolves. "Not that I'm surprised. You're a professional manipulator."

Rolling my eyes, I exhale. "Do you want the money or not?"

Her hand rests on her stomach briefly, and then she continues pacing. She's going to wear a beaten path into the wood floor by the time she's finished.

"Five million dollars." I fold my arms. "Final offer."

Mari stops in her tracks, her gaze flicking to mine. "I don't want to do this. I think it's a bad idea. But you're making it impossible for me to say no."

My mouth curls at the sides.

"I knew you'd see it my way." Moving to the door, I begin to show myself out, stopping to turn to her before I go. "My attorney will email you the pre-nuptial agreement. Please sign and return it by tomorrow, though if you'd like your attorney to go over it, I can give you an extra couple of days. Also, I'll clear my schedule Monday so I can take you shopping."

"Shopping?" Her head tilts.

"You'll need an engagement ring." I pull the

door wide and step into the hall. "My driver will pick you up at nine in the morning."

"O-okay." She blinks, eyes wide like she can't believe this is happening.

But I can.

I always get what I want.

But to be fair, my reward is more than worth worth her while. I may be a self-serving bastard, but I'm a generous self-serving bastard.

As long as she does whatever I say, whenever I say ... this little arrangement of ours will be a walk in the park.

Chapter Three

Mari

"I'm not going to call you 'sir' anymore." I climb into the backseat of his freshly waxed limousine Monday morning as it gently idles outside my apartment. The scent of supple leather and Hudson's Creed cologne fills my lungs with dizzying deliciousness the second I inhale. "I've been thinking about this all weekend." Obsessing, really. "I made of list of things I wanted to discuss with you before we dive into all of this. I have expectations too, you know. And I think it's really important that we—"

"Hot tea?" Hudson wears a warm smile as he hands me a paper cup with little tufts of steam rising from the lid. "You take yours with a splash of milk and one sugar. Or so I was told."

"Oh. Um. Thank you." I reach for the cup, my fingers brushing his. All things considered, this might be the kindest gesture this man's made toward me since I've known him.

I settle into my seat, my shoulders relaxing slightly. He's making an effort. This is good. This is a step in the right direction. This gives me hope that this thing might actually work out.

"Let me make one thing clear," I continue, blowing through the lid of my cup, eyes darting to him. "I'm in this for the money and only for the money. And I don't work for you. I'll be working with you. Side by side. Like a team. So don't treat me like your assistant anymore. Don't ask me to fetch you coffee or your dry cleaning. Even if I were your girlfriend or whatever, I wouldn't be running your errands. That's not my style."

His full lips arch into a coy smirk, but I have his attention. He's listening.

"In order for this to look authentic, it has to feel authentic," I say, placing my tea aside. "If it's me you want, it's me you're going to get—not some sugar substitute version."

The car stops outside a corner building, and an array of trademark red awning-covered windows catch my eye and silence my commentary.

"We're here," he says as his driver comes around to get the door.

I'm terribly underdressed for Cartier, but

Hudson doesn't say a word. He places his hand on the small of my back, leans into my ear, and whispers, "Try to keep it under six figures."

I nod, swallowing the nervous lump in my throat, and an armed man in a three-piece suit opens the front door with a welcoming smile.

"There he is!" a woman with shiny silver hair and a red, Jackie O style dress sashays toward us with open arms. "Hudson, my love. How are you? So good to see you. Come, come."

"Guinevere." He leans in for a hug, smiling as she air kisses his cheek, and then he reaches for my hand. "This is my beautiful fiancée, Maribel Collins."

Holding hands with Hudson Rutherford isn't something I imagined doing in a hundred billion years, but I clear my throat, throw my shoulders back, and walk in step past case beyond case of diamond jewels as we follow the lady in the red dress to a private elevator.

We arrive on the third level a moment later, the woman still rambling on. Apparently she knows Hudson's family well, having attended prep school with his mother decades ago.

"We're going to be in here today," she says,

trailing through a set of double mahogany doors. I'm guessing this building is some former old moneyed industrialist's turn of the century mansion, and this room looks like it doubled as a study or a library before it was converted to a private showroom. The walls are covered in dark polished board and batten, and the windows are tall and narrow, covered in fine draperies and letting in just enough natural light to send a dazzling glimmer to the curated displays of canary diamonds, emeralds, and sapphires lining the room. "You two have a seat. I'm going to grab a few pieces I pulled. I'll be right back."

Guinevere exits the room, pulling the doors closed behind her, and Hudson and I take our places in two red velvet chairs opposite an expansive desk.

We're still holding hands, and I don't know if he realizes that, but I don't move. Instead, I remind myself we're supposed to be "in love." This is what people who love each other do. They hold hands. They touch. They can't get enough of each other.

My stomach turns.

I don't know if it's the morning sickness or the fact that this is all happening so fast.

"All right." Guinevere returns, a case in her

hand covered in a red velvet cloth. She takes the seat on the other side of the desk and begins lining up the diamonds in size order, and just when I think they can't possibly get any bigger, she retrieves one last rock the size of my thumbnail and sits it on the end. "And I couldn't resist this guy. Just for fun. Eight flawless, cushion-cut carats."

She winks, flashing a smile in Hudson's direction.

"The bigger the better," I tease, squeezing his hand. "That's what I always say. Right, babe?"

"Love, I don't know." Guinevere pulls her glasses off her nose, placing them aside as she sighs. "You don't scream Park Avenue Princess to me. You seem very classic and understated. I wouldn't go more than three carats for you. This one might be too much, but here." She hands it over. "Go ahead and try it on."

I was only kidding, but I take the bauble and slip it down my left ring finger.

Fits like a glove.

I tilt my hand under the light, mesmerized by the fire and sparkle this thing throws. Guinevere is right. I'm not a flashy Park Avenue Princess, and I would *never* so much as put a ring like this on my wish list, but I'm playing a part. And I've seen the girls Hudson spends his spare time entertaining in his luxe penthouse. Girls like those love rings like these, I'm certain.

I am an actress ...

... and this is a prop.

It's that simple.

"Oh, baby, I love it!" I splay my hand across my chest and bat my lashes.

Hudson's eyes land on mine, like he's trying to silently ask me if I'm joking, but I don't let up.

"Isn't it beautiful?" I wave my hand in his face. "And eight carats! We met on the eighth of January. It's meant to be."

"It's a little ... much ... for your taste. Don't you think?" he asks carefully.

"Not. At. All." I pull the ring closer, inspecting it as if it's the most beautiful thing I've seen in my entire life. And maybe it is. "This is the one. I'm certain."

Guinevere sits up straight, her eyes dancing between the two of us as she keeps quiet, watching.

"Please?" I beg. The real Mari wouldn't beg.

It feels unnatural, like a dress that pulls at the shoulders or shoes that are too big in the toes.

"You really want this ring?" He lifts his left brow, rubbing his hand along his chiseled jaw.

I nod, clasping my hands together.

Hudson sighs, turning to Guinevere. "How much is this one going to set me back?"

She brings a finger to her lips, breathing in and exhaling. "Well. This one's special. It once belonged to the Duchess of Guildford in the 19th century. It's from our Legacy collection. I could show you a few pieces from our Estate collection if you'd like? Those are newer and less ... historically significant."

"Babe, this is a *royal* diamond." I place my hand on top of his, pouting. "This is a piece we could have in our family for generations to come. We could pass this down to our children's children someday. Could you even imagine?"

I hate the way I sound. Hate it.

Hudson sighs. "All right. You going to tell me how much it is?"

"Just a hair under two hundred," Guinevere says. "Comparable rings from our Estate collection would be quite less. I'm not sure what your budget is, but—"

"It's fine. We'll take it." Hudson reaches for my hand and squeezes—hard—before diving into his wallet and retrieving his black AmEx. "Anything for my future wife."

"You're a smart man, Hudson." Guinevere stands, collecting his card and the remainder of the engagement pieces. "And you're a very fortunate lady, Maribel. Hudson is one of New York's most eligible bachelors, and the Rutherfords are a wonderful family to marry into. Your parents must be proud."

"They're thrilled," I lie.

My parents have no idea, and ideally, I'd like to keep it that way.

They're salt-of-the-earth, childhood sweethearts who've never left their hometown of Orchard Hill, Nebraska. They're humble and kind. They go to St. Mary's for mass every Sunday and spend the weekends holed up in their Cornhusker-themed living room watching re-runs on HGTV.

They raised me to walk a straight line, to work hard, and to live a respectable life.

They wouldn't understand this.

And they sure as hell wouldn't be proud.

"Guinevere," Hudson says, "my parents don't know about the engagement yet, so if you could not mention it next time you see them ..."

"My lips are sealed. I promise. Be back in a moment." She smiles, slipping her glasses back over her nose and disappearing behind the double doors.

"Can you not?" Hudson turns to me, his expression fading the second she's gone.

"Not what?"

"Can you not act so vapid and materialistic? Eight carats? Are you fucking kidding me?" He rubs his temples and sinks back in his chair, staring straight ahead past one of the narrow windows. "And don't call me 'babe.' Please."

"I thought that's what you wanted?"

"What about me makes you think that's what I wanted?" His words are swift and frustrated.

"I don't know," I shrug. "I've seen the kind of women you associate with. I was just trying to be like them."

He huffs. "If I wanted a woman like that, I'd

have settled down a long time ago, Mari. There's a reason I chose you for this. You're not like them."

"What do you want me to do?" I lean forward, brows meeting in the middle. "Maybe you should've told me what you wanted from me before you brought me here. I'm not a mind reader. How do you want me to act?"

"Like yourself. Be authentic. Not a caricature."

I wrinkle my nose, readying my rebuttal just as Guinevere returns, two little red boxes in her hand. She slides the small ring box toward us.

"The ring fit you perfectly," she says to me. "Correct?"

I nod.

"Wonderful." She smiles, passing Hudson's card his way along with a receipt to sign. "And if you ever need it sized, please don't hesitate to bring it back. Also, as a special thank you, I'm throwing in a little something extra."

Guinevere slides the larger of the two boxes between us.

"It's a love bracelet," she says, cracking the box open with a gentle pop. A thick gold bangle rests on a velvet pillow alongside a matching gold screwdriver. "This is a signature piece. Very timeless and classic. Hudson, you're supposed to place it on her wrist and hold onto the screwdriver. You're the only one who can remove it."

My throat is dry. She may as well be presenting me with a medieval chastity belt. Who in their right mind would call this romantic?

"Wow," Hudson says. "Thank you. Mari, what do you think?"

I glance up, our eyes meeting, and I force an uneasy smile.

"I love it," I lie, hesitantly holding out my left wrist.

"Go on," Guinevere says, tucking her silver hair behind one ear. "Let me see it on you, love."

Hudson does the honors and within seconds I'm wearing a beautiful bracelet only he can remove. He slips the screwdriver into an interior pocket in his jacket before lifting my hand to his lips, depositing a kiss.

"Don't forget your ring!" Guinevere slides the ring box toward me. "It's a lovely piece. May it bring you a lifetime of happiness."

"Thank you." I slip the ring over my finger and drop the little red box in my purse. It's heavy and noticeable, something I didn't notice when I was too busy playing the part earlier. If I could go back thirty minutes, I'd have settled for something smaller and less ... Kardashian.

Too late.

"Shall we?" Hudson rises, extending his elbow, and I follow suit, slipping my hand under his arm. Guinevere shows us to the door, and I catch a glimpse of his limo waiting on the street corner.

His driver pops out, circling the idling car in a hurry and grabbing the door for us.

"Are you satisfied with your engagement ring?" Hudson asks a moment later, when we're cruising down Fifth Avenue and the privacy partition is raised.

I glance down. It doesn't shimmer as much in the dark. I guess it makes sense though— diamonds need light in order to shine.

"It's a beautiful ring," I say.

"Yes, but do you love it?"

"Does it matter?" I ask.

He doesn't answer. Instead, he checks his watch. "I'm going to head into the office. My driver will drop you off at Henri Bendel's where you're meeting with my stylist, Elle. She'll be choosing some pieces for you—for the summer in Montauk. I don't suppose you've ever been?"

I shake my head. "Nope."

"She's been instructed to outfit you with a few staples in addition to your Hamptons wardrobe."

"What's wrong with my current wardrobe?" I tilt my chin down, squinting. "You never had a problem with it at the office."

"I don't want you dressing like an assistant anymore."

"I thought you wanted me to be myself?" I glance down at my gray slacks and white blouse.

"I do want you to be yourself." He reaches across the empty middle seat and places his hand over mine. "But I'd love for you to dress the part."

"That's right. I forgot you have an eye for design." I roll my eyes when he's not looking.

"Design is everything. Aesthetics are everything." He glances out the window to his right, his hand remaining on mine. I recognize the street ahead. We're getting closer to the office. This time last week, I was scrambling around ordering lunch for some English architects he decided to host at his office at the last minute. When it was over, he told me I should have chosen a better restaurant, one for more sophisticated palates.

"Beauty is only skin deep."

The car comes to a slow stop outside Rutherford Architectural's building.

"I give zero fucks about beauty." He turns to me. "Design? That's what matters. When you look at a building or a piece of art and it makes you feel something? That's design. Someone intentionally created their piece with the sole purpose of making you feel something when you look at it. Beauty is secondary. Beauty is the stone or the marble or the fabric. The interpretation of the design."

"I don't understand what this has to do with the way I dress."

"You're a beautiful woman, Mari," he says. "And if you're going to be mine, I won't have you hiding beneath cheap design. I'm upgrading your wardrobe effective immediately."

I laugh. "Why? So you can feel something

59

when you look at me?"

The driver opens Hudson's door, but Hudson stays, letting his gaze linger on mine as we bask in temporary silence. He doesn't answer me. He simply steps out a second later.

Straightening his suit jacket, he runs a hand down his thin black tie before leaning down to meet my gaze one last time.

"Elle will take good care of you today." His lips press together and he exhales through his nose. "I'll pick you up around one for lunch."

"Oh? I had no idea. I'm supposed to meet one of my friends then. You have to tell me these things in advance."

"You'll need to reschedule."

"I said I'd help you out, Hudson. I didn't say you could commandeer my entire life."

"I'm not commandeering anything. We need to have a date. We need to get to know each other. Soon you'll be accompanying me to Montauk for the month of June, which means we need to be spending every spare moment together until then."

I exhale, my fingers spinning the ridiculous ring on my finger.

"See you at one," he says before turning to leave.

The driver closes the door and returns to the front, and I grab my phone, texting my best friend, Isabelle, to ask for a rain check and promising to explain everything as soon as I can.

Settling back against the smooth leather seat, I stare at Manhattan through a tinted window, placing my hand on my lower belly.

"I'm doing this for you, baby," I whisper.

Chapter Four

Hudson

Mari climbs into the backseat as my driver loads her bags into the trunk.

"Hi." She tucks a strand of blonde hair behind one ear, brushing her hands along the back of her skirt-covered thighs.

That's new.

I scan her from head to toe.

Her hair is lighter than before, parted deep on one side and slightly curled, and her lips are slicked in deep cherry red. A willowy blouse cut low in the front clings to her shoulders.

She looks ... chic. Effortlessly classy. And I can't take my fucking eyes off her.

"You look nice," I say, my mouth forming a crooked smirk as I allow my gaze to linger a bit longer than usual.

She smooths her hand over a loose tendril. "Thanks. Got a bit of a makeover today. You were right about Elle. She's got a great eye. And thank you for the clothes. I agree ... my wardrobe was in dire need of an upgrade."

There's a gleam in Mari's blue eyes that I didn't expect. A veiled smile too. Already I can see she's carrying herself differently. A little more charm? A little more grace? A little more confidence than before? Not that she was lacking. I'd always thought of Mari as somewhat of a quiet storm; assertive, beautiful, and potentially destructive if not properly handled.

It isn't her fault though. It's her age—her generation. They want the world at the snap of their entitled little fingertips. They want it all and they want it yesterday.

But they're not ready.

One minute they're giving world-class presentations in boardrooms and the next minute they're hurling tantrums like a teething toddler when something doesn't go their way.

This experience will be good for Mari. I think she's really going to hit her stride under my wing, and when it's over, she'll find herself a little more refined, a little more patient, and she'll find the world is a little more within her reach than it was before.

"I hope you're not too hungry. I moved our reservations so we could make a little stop on the way," I say, checking my watch.

"Where are we going?"

"Your apartment. Then the restaurant."

"And why are we stopping at my apartment?" Her nose wrinkles.

"You'll see soon enough."

Mari crosses her long legs and slides back into the seat as we merge into the busy mid-day traffic. Within a half hour, we're sitting outside her building, parked behind a moving truck.

Leaning forward, she squints toward the uniformed men lugging furniture pieces up a ramp.

"That looks like my ..." her voice trails off. "That's ... is that my dresser?"

Reaching for the door handle, she scurries to climb out of the limo. I follow, placing my hand on her shoulder as she stares wide-eyed as her things are loaded.

"What are you doing with my things?" She

turns to me. "And how did you get access to my apartment?"

"You're moving in with me."

"And why wasn't this communicated with me?" She whips her gaze in my direction, her hands landing on her hips.

"It was. Didn't you read the contract you signed over the weekend?"

"Of course I read it."

"Then surely you read the fine print?" I ask.

Her expression wilts as she glances over my shoulder and into the distance.

"Pretty sure I would've noticed a cohabitation clause," she says, chewing on the inside of her lip. Mari exhales, and I watch in real time as her frustration seems to be redirected at herself.

"Either way, it's a done deal. It's happening. You're living with me—in the guest suite of course," I say. "It's important that we get to know each other's habits—our idiosyncrasies, if you will. We need to have some kind of authentic semblance of a relationship. It can't all be acting. Now, go upstairs and collect your personal belongings.

Everything else will go into storage. I'll wait here in the car."

Mari exhales, saying nothing before she turns on her heels and shimmies between two movers carrying oversized crates of her pre-Rutherford life.

Smirking, I climb back into the car.

I knew I chose well.

Chapter Five

Mari

"If you need anything, dial seven on your phone. Marta will be able to assist you. I'll be in my study. You're welcome to join me once you're settled in."

Hudson disappears, closing my bedroom door behind him, and I bask in the surrealness of this moment. One minute I'm quitting my job, the next minute I'm plucked from my world, given a *Pretty Woman*-esque makeover and a lavish bedroom suite easily twice the size of my shoebox apartment.

Circling the room, I pass by the east window, taking in the view of the city from what feels like the top of the world. It's raining now, little drops beading against the crystal clear glass. Two bedside lamps flank a king-sized bed fit for a spread in Metropolitan Home magazine, and I run to the foot, sinking down in the middle. The bedding is cashmere soft and smells faintly of lavender linen spray.

A knock at my door pulls me from this magical moment, and I scramble to my feet.

"Yes, come in," I call.

The door swings open and Hudson's driver stands there, Henri Bendel bags in his arms.

"Your things, Miss Collins," he says.

I step out of the way, ushering him in. For a moment, I'd forgotten all about today's shopping excursion. I've never been a materialistic person, and I never want to be. But nothing beats having a personal stylist pulling pieces shaped for my body type in colors meant to flatter my hair and skin. If it weren't for Elle, I never would have known that fuchsia was my color. And if it weren't for Manuel at the Fekkai salon, I never would've thought lopping a couple of inches off my hair and changing up my part would alter my entire look for the better.

On this ordinary Monday, this modest Midwestern girl was queen for the day, and I'll never forget it as long as I live.

"Thank you, Rocco," I say when he returns with another armful of bags, placing them near the dresser.

A few minutes later, dozens of paper shopping bags cover the hardwood floor, and I hum softly to myself as I hang my new wardrobe in the walk-in closet and organize about a dozen shoeboxes along wooden shelves.

When I'm finished, I pass the dresser, catching my reflection in the mirror. At first pass, it doesn't immediately register that the girl staring back … is me. I stop, giving myself a curious glance. Twisting a tendril of hair and tucking it behind my ear, my gaze falls on my faded red lips. The day is already starting to wear off, and the second I strip out of this Dior pencil skirt and Chanel blouse and wash the rest of this makeup off my face, my Cinderella moment will be over.

But that's okay.

I don't want this experience to change me.

I'm fine the way I am. I like myself, unlike most women I know who are my age. And besides, when I move back to Nebraska and have my baby, no one's going to care which labels fill my closet or whether or not my shoes have red bottoms.

Turning to leave, I hit the light switch on my way out and stride down the hall toward Hudson's study.

He's right. We have to spend time together and get to know each other's annoying little habits. One erroneous statement and this entire thing could come skidding to a halt, and then all of this will have been for nothing.

I pass a portrait gallery, one I've never noticed before. I've roamed these halls dozens of times before, always dropping off his dry cleaning or signing for packages when Marta's out running errands. Never once did I envision myself living here. The faces staring back in the photographs must be his family. And soon they'll be my family — at least on paper.

Weird.

Everything feels brand new, like I'm seeing this place for the first time all over again: the view of the city from his living room windows, the glossy marble kitchen, the floor-to-ceiling fireplace, the custom chandelier in his foyer. Every square inch of this place was planned with purpose and intention, which isn't surprising considering Hudson's eye for detail.

Making my way to his study, I linger in the doorway and watch him work. He doesn't notice me. He's far too concerned with the sketch he's working on, placing the pencil between his full lips at times and dragging his hands through his hair.

I've never taken the time to watch him work—at least not like this.

He's actually kind of sexy when he's in the zone, all serious and contemplative.

"Don't they make software that does that for you?" I interrupt his focus with a playful question.

He drops his drafting pencil. "My computer's at the office. Besides, even the best CAD program is no substitute for some good, old-fashioned hand-sketching."

He rises, presenting his paper in my direction. It appears to be a home of some kind, one with vintage familiarity that would look perfectly content resting on a beachfront lot.

"What's that for?" I ask. I've only ever seen him work on commercial projects.

"My cousin has tasked me with designing her Cape Cod estate," he says. "What do you think?"

I move closer, taking the paper from his hands and examining it carefully. "I don't know the proper terms for any of these things, but I like the roof lines. And I like the shake siding. I think it's called shake, right? And I like how the front porch wraps around the house so you can always find a shady place to sit no matter where the sun is in the sky. The double front doors are a nice touch, and those little windows above the garage. It's homey yet it makes a statement. If I were driving past this house, I think I'd slow down a little and take a longer look."

"Perfect." He takes the paper back. "That's exactly what I'm going for."

Placing his drawing aside, he grabs a jacket from the back of his office chair and slips it over his shoulders.

"Where are you going?" I ask.

"Out." He lifts a brow, adjusting his sleeves and straightening his posture.

"I thought you said we needed to spend time together?"

"I'm just grabbing a couple of drinks, Mari. It's my Monday night ritual. The Cypress Taproom on Houston has a table reserved for me."

"I don't care if the Queen of England has a table reserved for you at Buckingham Palace … you're not going out without me." I fight a smart-assed grin, letting my words slice through his cold demeanor. "You want authentic, Hudson? This is authentic. I'm your girlfriend now. Fiancée. Whatever. You can't go out for drinks and leave me at home. It's rude. People in relationships don't do that."

He smirks, rubbing his jaw. "I suppose you have a point."

"I know I have a point," I spit my words. "You don't get to pull me out of my world, dress me up like some doll, and sit me on a shelf in your apartment until you're ready to play with me. If we're going to do this, let's do this."

Hudson places a palm in the air. "Don't lecture me, Mari. Please. It's inappropriate."

"What's inappropriate is the fact that you insisted I move in with you immediately because we needed to spend as much time together as possible and the second I was settled in, you were going to run out of here to grab some drinks by yourself."

"Point. Taken." His jaw clenches, his gaze steely. "Forgive me. Old habits die hard. Not accustomed to my social obligations being attached to anyone else's. Would you like to join me?"

"No thanks." Not that I could if I wanted to anyway. I hold my chin high. "We're staying in tonight. Like a regular, boring couple."

His expression fades. Clearly the idea doesn't appeal to him.

"Have you ever had a girlfriend, Hudson? Like a serious, long-term relationship?" I ask.

"Once," he says. "In college. It was awful."

I chuckle. "Figures."

"So what do we do now?" he asks.

Sighing, I glance up at the ceiling and deduce that there's only one appropriate plan of action in this moment.

"You're going to have to teach me how to live in your world," I say, "and I'll teach you how to be a good fiancé."

Hudson smirks. "Obviously. I meant what do we do now ... as in tonight."

"Oh." My cheeks warm. "Right. We could change into some comfortable clothes and sit on the couch and watch Netflix?"

He stares straight ahead, unable to mask the disgust on his face.

"What's wrong with that?" I ask. "Don't you

ever just zone out and binge watch some really addictive TV?"

"I don't have time for … *Netflix*."

"You do now." I take him by the arm and lead him to his living room. "Where's your TV?"

"Not in here."

"I forgot. Rich people don't keep their TVs in plain view." I roll my eyes, releasing my hand from his arm. "Is it in your room?"

"I have one in the master suite, yes," he says. "I'll have to see if I can find the remote. Not sure where Marta put it …"

"Okay, go find it. I'm going to change out of this skirt and into something I can lounge around in. And you should too. I'll meet you in your room in ten minutes, and then we're watching *Orange is the New Black*."

"*Orange is the new* what?"

"It's a show. You'll like it. Trust me." I stifle my laughter. The idea of Hudson Rutherford watching a bunch of imprisoned women fuck each other over (and occasionally fuck each other) makes me giggle. It's *so* not his style, but damn is that show addictive.

Padding back to my suite, I close the door behind me and change into a set of matching silk pajamas—navy with white piping—and wash up for bed. When I'm almost finished, my phone buzzes on the dresser.

My best friend.

"Hey, Isabelle," I answer. "What's up?"

"Are you okay? You never cancel on me."

"Everything's fine." I purse my lips together. She's never going to believe this.

"Is it the baby?" she asks.

I place my hand on my belly. I've been so caught up in everything today that I almost forgot …

"The baby's fine," I whisper.

"Why'd you cancel?"

"I've accepted a new assignment from my boss." I bite my lower lip and squeeze my eyes, waiting for her lecture. "It's kept me a little … occupied."

"You said you were going to quit." Isabelle sighs into the receiver. "That asshole doesn't deserve you. You do way too much for him and for what? A laughable salary? Underhanded insults? And you said you caught him staring at your ass once. What a fucking unprofessional douche. Never even met the guy and I hate him."

"He wants me to marry him," I whisper.

Isabelle is quiet on the other end. That's never a good sign.

"It's a business arrangement," I say. "He's basically paying me to take him off the market."

"Um, why?" Her voice is laced with irritation. She's not going to understand, so I'm going to have to make this crystal clear.

"His parents are pressuring him to marry some girl and he doesn't want to. So he's marrying me instead. I'm spending the summer with him and his family and then we're going our separate ways. At least physically. Legally we'll be married for a while. Not sure how long. It's all kind of complicated and it's all happening so fast."

"Mari, you can't do this."

"I thought so too, but he sweetened the pot pretty damn good, and I'm not exactly in a position to walk away from what he was offering."

"Fine. Sell your soul."

"Izzy." My heart sinks. This isn't like her. I know she means well, and I know I've filled her head with hundreds of Hudson Rutherford horror stories, but I need her support now more than ever. "Please understand. I'm doing this for my future—for the baby's future. I'm not selling my soul. He's not forcing me to do this. It's really not that big of a deal at the end of the day. It's just acting. I'm playing a part. Everything's going to work out."

"And what if it doesn't?" she asks.

"I … I don't know?"

"What are you going to do if someone discovers that you're not really in love, that you're faking this relationship? What if it blows up in your faces? And oh, my God, Mari. Does he know you're pregnant?!"

I exhale. "No."

"Mari! Why didn't you tell him? Holy shit. This is bad. This is really, really bad."

"Izzy, stop. It'll be fine. I'm five-foot-nine. I doubt I'll be showing much by the end of the summer, and I'll just wear billowy tops and flowy dresses. It's not like he's going to see me naked. We're not taking it that far."

"You're being *wayyyy* too optimistic about

this."

"For five million dollars, wouldn't you be optimistic about this?!" I ask, my voice quick and hushed.

She's quiet once more.

"He's paying you five million dollars to be his fake wife?" Isabelle asks.

"Yep."

"There's got to be a catch," she says.

"Nope. No catch. He's just a desperate man with deep pockets."

"Well. Shit. Um. Okay. Yeah. Do your thing. I hope it all works out for you. And if you need me, I'll be here."

"Really? I have your support?" I ask.

"Do you even have to ask that, Mar? You're my best friend. You could do a lot worse than fake-marrying your asshole boss and I'd still have your back."

"For a minute it sounded like you were trying to talk me out of this."

"Of course I was trying to talk you out of

this. I think it's insane. I think it's a terrible idea. And I think it could potentially end very badly for you. But for five million dollars, I guess you have to do what you have to do."

"It's definitely a gamble," I say. "But we're doing it. I've signed the contract. It's happening."

"There's a contract?"

"Of course." I pull my phone from my ear and check the time. "Anyway, he's expecting me in his room right now, so I'm going to let you go. Call me tomorrow?"

"In his room?" She ignores me. "I thought you said you weren't going to have sex with him?"

"I'm not. We're going to watch Netflix," I say.

"A week ago you hated this guy. Hated him. And now you're going to chill in his bed and watch TV." Isabelle exhales. "This is just ... weird."

"Wait 'til you see the engagement ring. I'll send you a picture later," I laugh. "It's *so* over the top and *so* not me and you're going to die."

"I can only imagine."

Chapter Six

Hudson

"You look uncomfortable." Mari pulls her legs up to her chest, her body covered in satin pajamas with white trim. "Can you do me a favor and not make this any more awkward than it already is?"

I scoff. "I'm not making it awkward."

I've managed to find the remote, and the TV quietly rises from the foot of the bed. Good to see it still works.

"You are. You're all the way over on that side of the bed." She points. "And I'm over here. Not that I want to, but maybe I should be lying in your arms?"

Her forehead wrinkles, but she seems to be waiting for me to make the next move.

"All right. Fine," I say, pulling up the covers. I place my arm out and motion for her to scoot closer.

Mari doesn't hesitate making herself right at home, nuzzling against me, her head resting on my shoulder as we sink into the pillows behind us. I don't think I've ever held a woman like this—at least not in a non-sexual way and not since college.

"Where's your remote?" she asks.

I hand it over, watching as she maneuvers the guide like a pro and manages to pull up Netflix and log in. Within a minute, some opening credits are playing and a bunch of women's faces are flashing on the screen. The lighting is garish and the music is high-tempo and obnoxious, but I keep my opinion to myself. Something tells me it wouldn't matter with her anyway.

"You smell good," Mari says quietly, turning to me.

"What?"

"I like your cologne. I've always liked it. Just never had the chance to tell you."

"Thanks." I offer a half-smile. "I've worn it for years. It's my signature scent."

"I've never known a man who had a signature scent before," she says, though I think she's teasing. "Does it help with your energy?"

"I beg your pardon?"

"I'm messing with you." She shoves me gently. "You're always talking about how things mess with your creative energy." Mari swats her hand. "Never mind. It was funnier in my head."

"I'm sure it was." I roll my eyes. "Why don't we watch this show that you insisted was so addictive?"

"Do you think we should hold hands?" she asks a few minutes later, just as I was actually becoming slightly invested in what's happening on the screen.

"My arm is around you."

"Obviously," she says, exhaling. "But maybe we should hold hands? After a while, maybe it'll actually start to feel natural? You know, every boyfriend I've ever had couldn't keep his hands off me, and here I have to basically remind you that you should be touching me."

"I'm not like those other men."

"Clearly."

"I'm not the touchy-feely type," I say. "Never have been."

"That's too bad." I feel her eyes on me. "You know, studies have shown that when you touch someone, it stimulates these feel-good hormones or endorphins or something like that. Human touch is powerful. Sometimes it can even trick your brain into thinking you're in love."

My gaze snaps to hers. "The last thing I need is my brain insisting I'm in love with my fake wife."

"Trust me, Hudson," she says, half-smiling. "You're not going to fall in love with me. I won't allow it."

Chapter 7

Mari

"Heartbeat is strong. Measurements look good. I'd say you're about six weeks and two days." The strawberry-blonde nurse replaces the sonogram Doppler and snaps off her latex gloves before rising. "Congratulations. The doctor will be in shortly to answer any questions you may have."

She leaves, flicking the light back on before closing the door, and Isabelle glances across the room at me. She didn't have to come, but she insisted that I not be alone.

"So have you decided what you're going to do?" she asks.

"I'm keeping it."

"I know that. I mean, like, are you going to stick around the city? I hear Brooklyn's pretty family friendly," she says.

"No." I climb off the exam table and move toward the sink, grabbing a paper towel to clean the gunk from my belly. "I can't afford to raise a baby in the city. I'll have to go back home, maybe live with my parents until I can get on my feet. Maybe move to Omaha and find a job in the city? You know what they say, Omaha is the new Manhattan."

"Nobody says that," Isabelle chuckles, brushing her shiny onyx hair away from her face. "Speaking of your parents, have you told them yet?"

I shake my head, biting my lip. "Not yet."

"When are you going to tell them?"

"Soon."

"You kill me with your fly-by-the-seat-of-your-pants existence. I've never met anyone who lives in the moment as much as you do." Isabelle grabs her phone from her purse and checks the time.

"I like to think that's a good thing." I shrug. "I find life's a whole lot easier when you take it one day at a time."

"I don't know how you do it."

Dr. Gupta raps three times on the door before padding in, a tablet in hand and a stethoscope around her neck. Her eyes dance between the two of us before I head back to the exam table.

"How are you feeling, Maribel?" she asks.

"A little nauseous, a little tired. But otherwise good," I answer.

"Are you taking your prenatals? Prenatal vitamins?"

"Just started last week."

"Good, good," she says, nails clicking on her tablet. "So you're six weeks and two days, which would put your due date at January sixth of next year."

"Oh, wow." It seems so close, yet so far away. And slapping an actual due date on it makes it all the more real.

"Did the nurse talk to you about our classes? We have everything from childbirth techniques to caring for newborns to parenting."

"She gave me some pamphlets," I say.

"I highly recommend them. You can bring your partner too." She glances at Isabelle.

"Oh, she's not my—"

"I'll be there," Isabelle says with a smile, giving me an emerald-eyed wink. I love her.

"Do you have any questions for me?" Dr. Gupta asks, eyeing the door. For some reason, I expected this to take longer. I guess it never dawned on me that people get pregnant every day, and I'm not some special snowflake pregnant lady who needs to hoard all of the good doctor's time.

I shake my head. "None that I can think of."

"Well, everything looks great on the ultrasound. Why don't you stop by the lab on your way out so we can get a quick draw on you, okay? We'll check a few levels and give you a call if anything looks amiss. Just some standard tests we run on all of our pregnant patients."

"Sure."

"Great, Maribel." She places her hand on my shoulder on her way to the door. "We'll see you back in late June for your twelve-week ultrasound."

With that, Dr. Gupta leaves.

"You hungry?" Isabelle asks, rising and gathering her things.

"Always."

"The usual place?"

I nod.

"You okay?" she asks. "You're quiet all of a sudden."

Smiling, I say, "Just letting it all sink in. Doesn't feel real. Not even with the heartbeat and the due date."

"Once you start showing, maybe it'll feel real? Or maybe once you feel it kick?" Isabelle puts her arm around me as we head to the door.

"Maybe?"

"Are you going to find out what it is?" she asks. "Wait, what the hell kind of question is that. Of course you aren't."

I laugh. "You know me well."

Chapter Eight

Hudson

"I'd like to meet your parents, Mari." I pour her a glass of red wine over a candlelit dinner Friday evening at a romantic Michelin star restaurant on the Upper East Side, Villa Moreno's. We haven't seen much of each other this week as I've been working longer hours than usual finishing up plans for a public library in Still Creek Township, New Jersey, but it's time to get back on track.

Reaching for the nearest glass of water, she tosses back a couple gulps in an attempt to disguise a startled choke.

"You never said anything about meeting my parents," she says when she comes up for air. "I really don't want to involve them in any of this. I can't do that to them."

I take a sip of my wine, swirling it first, then flashing a million-dollar smile. "Why wouldn't they be a part of this? I'm marrying their daughter."

"You're fake-marrying their daughter, which means you're going to be my fake husband and they're going to be your fake in-laws. It's probably better off that they don't even meet you."

"Why's that?"

She sighs. "Honestly, you're probably not what they had in mind for me. And I don't even know if they'll like you. And if they think I'm marrying someone who doesn't deserve me, it'll break their hearts."

"Ouch."

"I'm just being honest, Hudson." She takes another sip of water, completely ignoring the hundred-dollar glass of pinot placed before her. "You're not personable or friendly. You're not small town. You're cold and distant and self-important. You're all business and no fun. They've got pretty high hopes, and I don't think they'd be crazy about their only child growing up to become some fancy-pants architect's trophy wife."

"A *fancy-pants architect's trophy wife?*" I chuckle. "Is that all you think you're going to be to me?"

She nods. "Basically."

"Just as your parents have expectations for

your future partner, mine do too. My mother would choke on her pearls if she believed all I wanted for a life partner was some vapid trophy wife. I'm looking for an equal, Mari. Someone intelligent. Respectable. Strong. A force to be reckoned with." My eyes lock on hers. "And that's you. All you have to do is be yourself, and my parents will love you and think you're absolutely perfect for me."

Mari clears her throat, glancing down at the napkin folded in her lap. "Wow. Um. That's … that's really nice of you to say … I kind of feel bad now."

"Don't. You were only being honest. I respect an honest woman." I take another sip of wine.

Our server approaches the table, taking our orders, and my gaze falls on Mari's still untouched wine goblet.

"Not feeling wine tonight?" I ask.

She shakes her head. "Not really a drinker. Sorry."

"I never knew that about you."

"There are a lot of things you don't know about me." She flashes a smile that, for a split second, makes me feel like I've known her a lot longer than two months. "At least not yet."

I lift my wine, nodding toward her water glass. "A toast?"

She clinks her drink against mine.

"To getting to know one another," I say.

"To getting to know one another," she mimics.

I take another sip, unable to remove my gaze from her. Under the flickering candlelight, she's radiant, glowing from within. Her blonde hair is swept back, just off her neck, and subtle diamond studs adorn her ears. Her lips are shaded in soft pink and her lashes are dark and curled. She's the image of whispered grace and emerging refinement wrapped in a tight little black dress and heels that make her almost as tall as me.

She's going to fit in just fine as the newest member of the Rutherford family.

Not a doubt in my mind.

Placing my hand across the table, I bring it over hers. Our eyes meet once more.

"You look beautiful tonight, Mari," I say. "I meant to tell you that earlier when I picked you up."

"Thank you." Her full lips press together, stifling a humbled smile.

Suddenly and without warning, I find myself desperately curious to know what they taste like, what they feel like. And when Mari readjusts her posture, bending forward, the pillow-soft tops of her breasts nearly spill out of her dress, sending my cock straining against the inside of my slacks.

Thank God for table cloths.

"Anyway, how was your day?" she asks, head tilted to the side.

But I can't think about my day, and mind-numbing small talk doesn't interest me. All I can do is stare at the sexy little thing in front of me. And knowing sex is completely off the table and that I'm literally the last person on earth Mari would ever want to fuck only makes me want her more.

Chapter Nine

Mari

"My mom hugs," I say as he stretches next to the kitchen island early Saturday morning. Last night we shared a candlelit dinner uptown, and in the car on the way home, he reached for my hand, taking it in his. I didn't even have to remind him to touch me, he just did it on his own. "Like, a lot. Don't say I didn't warn you."

"I think I can handle her."

"Her name is Margo," I say. "My dad is Abel. That's why they named me Maribel."

"Adorable," he chuffs.

"They've been together since they were fourteen."

He kicks a leg behind him, grabbing his ankle and stretching out his quad before repeating it on the other side. When Hudson eyes the clock and grabs a bottle of Smart water from the fridge, I feel guilty for not joining him.

I ate like a heifer last night—a pregnant heifer, that is. I ate three-fourths of the Italian bread loaf on the table plus my kale salad before polishing off an entire dish of chicken marsala and suggesting to Hudson that we split a piece of chocolate raspberry cake.

He didn't say a word though, bless his cold little heart.

"My dad will probably want to talk to you about college football. Or tools. Or cars," I say as he makes his way to the door. "So ... study up."

"Will do." He smirks. I don't believe him. "Going for a quick run. Be back in a half hour."

"Okay ... I'll ... be here."

Marta scurries into the kitchen the second he's gone, fishing a small kit of cleaning supplies from under the sink. With a focused fury, she begins polishing the already-pristine counters and wiping off the already mirror-like stainless appliances.

"Want some help?" I offer. It feels weird just sitting here at the island doing nothing while she cleans like her life depends on it. I haven't lifted a finger since I got here a few days ago, and it seems wrong.

"No, no." Marta waves her hand, scrubbing the immaculate counters with a blue rag. "You relax, Miss Collins. I'm just doing my job."

Ever since Hudson let her in on the plan and informed her I was moving in, she's been acting different around me.

"You don't have to call me Miss Collins," I say. "Just a week ago, I was his assistant and you were calling me Mari."

"Yes," she says. "And now you live here. I work for Mr. Rutherford and I work for you. Formalities are expected in this home."

"You don't work for me." I laugh. The idea of me with a servant is ridiculous. "You don't even have to clean my room if you don't want."

"Yes, I do," she snaps. And I realize that perhaps it was offensive for me to suggest she isn't needed or for me to come in here and undermine the man who cuts her paychecks. "I have a system, Miss Collins. I clean the bathrooms on Mondays, Wednesdays, and Fridays. The bedrooms every other day, all floors once a day, and—"

"It's fine." I place a hand up. "Totally understand that you have a routine. I was just trying to lighten your load."

Marta stops scrubbing and glances up at me. "I love my job, Miss Collins. Mr. Rutherford is good to me, and I try my best to be good to him in return. You won't find a speck of dust in this place or an ounce of spoiled food in the fridge, I can promise you that."

Hudson is good to her? Never would've guessed that.

I watch Marta move from the marble to the stainless to the interior of the microwave and beyond before sliding off the bar stool and tiptoeing back to my suite. I've never known Marta to be so distant to me before.

It's almost as if she doesn't like me now.

Just weeks ago, we were joking about how particular Hudson is about which dry cleaner he uses right down to the brand of starch they keep on hand, and now she's acting like we're strangers.

My stomach rolls when I get back to my room, and I collapse onto the squishy, cashmere-soft bed I've come to love these last few nights. I'm either hungry or I have to throw up—maybe both, but I'm too exhausted to move.

Reaching for my phone on the nightstand, I check my usual apps out of boredom before mindlessly pulling up Safari and heading over to a baby name blog. I've been doing that lately ... thinking about what I'm going to name this little babe.

My plan is to wait until I meet it, see what it looks like, and go from there. But I'd like to have a few options or a short list or something to pull from.

Pulling up my messages, I shoot Isabelle a text.

Me: Adelia?

Her: Nope.

Me: Nuriel?

Her: Pass!!

Me: Cammelia?

Her: Idk... maybe.

Me: Zasarn?

Her: Are you naming a baby or an alien? Seriously, Mar.

Chuckling, I go back to the blog and scan

for some new names to pester her with. I like to mix it up and make her think I'm going to name this thing something way out of the left field. Keep her on her toes a bit.

Rolling to my back, I brush my messy hair from my face. I need to shower. I need to get cleaned up and find something productive to do today. I hate not working, but I guess, in a way, this is my job for a while. And it's pointless to get back out there and search for something when I'm going to be moving back to Nebraska at the end of summer anyway.

There's a slight rap on the door, which sends a quick shock through my middle.

"Yeah?" I call out.

"Miss Collins?" It's Marta. Maybe she's coming to apologize? Or empty my bathroom trash. It could really go either way at this point. "We have a visitor."

My stomach sinks. I don't know what to do with a visitor. Should I have her start some tea? Set out some macaroons? Do I greet them in the study or the living room?

Shuffling out of bed and across the room, I pull the door open.

"Is Hudson back from his run yet?" I ask.

Marta shakes her head.

"Who is it?" I ask.

"His mother."

"Oh." I bite my lip, feeling the pulse of blood as it rushes to my head. Was not expecting that. "Okay. I just need to get cleaned up and I'll—"

"She doesn't like to be kept waiting." Marta looks me up and down. She doesn't say it, but she doesn't need to. I look a hot mess.

Lovely.

"Five minutes," I say, shutting the door and scrambling toward the bathroom.

Tugging on a pair of barely worn jeans from yesterday and a white blouse, I pat some tinted moisturizer onto my face, swipe on some mascara and blush, and dab a bit of sheer, rose-hued lipstick over my lips to finish it off. Combing my hair back, I tie it into a low bun before spritzing on a modest amount of some fancy perfume with a name I can't even begin to pronounce.

I'm done in a hair over seven minutes. Close enough. And definitely a record for me.

With my heart whooshing in my ears, I make my way down the hall, toward the foyer where a woman with jet-black hair that stops at her elegant jawline, a swan-like neck, thick pearls, and a pink Chanel dress waits. Her hands are clasped in front of her, a Dior clutch dangling from her manicured fingertips.

"Hello," I say. I muster a warm smile and walk toward her, extending my right hand. "You're Hudson's mother? It's nice to meet you."

Her gaze falls to my right hand, and she pauses before meeting it with her own. She's hesitant of me. Or maybe she's in shock, trying to wrap her head around why some strange woman she's never met is staying at her son's place while he's out and about.

"Yes. Helena Rutherford," she says with a reluctant smile. "And you are?"

"Mari," I say again. "Mari Collins."

"Lovely to meet you, Mari." She squints, studying me. "And who are you in relation to my son?"

"Oh. Right." My heart thumps hard before falling to my feet. I don't know how to answer this. I wasn't supposed to meet her this soon. I don't even know if he's mentioned me yet, and I don't want to screw this up. "I'm his—"

Helena sucks in a shocked gasp of breath, reaching for my left hand. It didn't take her long to spot the engagement ring.

Oh, shit …

My jaw hangs. I'm searching for the words, willing myself to say something—anything—but I'm at a loss. I'm nothing but a wordless, speechless idiot.

The soft click of the door lock pulls our attention away and by some stroke of magic, Hudson wanders in like a sweat-glistened knight in shining gym shorts. Sweat dampens his shirt collar and his dark hair is wet, finger-combed back. He looks like he just walked off a Nike billboard in Times Square whereas anytime I work out, I tend to resemble a sewer rat by the time I'm finished.

"Mother." He stops in his tracks, accepting a fluffy towel Marta brings to him and wiping his brow. "What are you doing here?"

"I was in the city," she says, her tone flatter than it was a moment ago. "Thought I'd stop by and pay you a visit."

He approaches her, pressing a quick kiss

into her check. "Wonderful. In that case, I take it you've just met my fiancée?"

Helena swallows, her smooth jaw tighter than her creaseless forehead. "I have now."

Hudson smiles. "I was planning to make the announcement this summer, but since you're here … meet Maribel Collins, my future wife."

I nod and smile, forcing myself to stare at Hudson like he hung the moon before glancing back into his mother's distant brown stare. The apple certainly doesn't fall far from the tree in the Rutherford family.

And I have no idea what he was talking about when he claimed all I had to do was be myself and his parents would love me. Judging by his mother's icy demeanor, she's either in shock or having an internal conniption at this very moment.

I take his side, slipping my arm into his and gazing into his sapphire irises.

"I can't wait to marry your son, Mrs. Rutherford." I turn back to her. "He's everything I could ever hope for in a partner. Intelligent. Ambitious. Hardworking. They don't make them like him anymore."

"How long have you two …?" His mother's

105

gaze passes between us.

"Not long," I answer.

"I met her in January," he lies. "I'm afraid it was a case of love at first sight. Who'd have thought that was actually a thing?"

"Right," his mother echoes softly, as though she's lost in her own thoughts. "Who'd have thought?"

Hudson leans down, kissing the top of my head. "I can't wait for you to get to know Mari this summer, Mother. She's as beautiful inside as she is out."

Helena watches us with careful, scrutinizing regard before snapping out of it and clearing her throat.

"Yes, yes," she says, a smile returning to her shock-white expression. Her eyes come alive, and it's as if she flipped a switch. "Well, I suppose congratulations are in order. Hudson, I take it you'll call your father and share the news before we head to Montauk? You know how he absolutely despises being the last to know."

"Of course," he says.

"We'll plan a little celebration. An

engagement party, if you will. Something small," she says, heading toward the door then stopping to turn back. I find it interesting that she suddenly has somewhere to go. Maybe she needs to process this? "I'm sure the Sheffields will be tickled pink." Her eyes graze my body, top to bottom. "Audrina in particular." She chuckles to herself, shaking her head as if she finds something humorous.

Tilting her head high, she marches toward the door, her red-bottomed heels clicking on his marble foyer tile.

The second she's gone, I glance at Hudson.

"She hates me already," I say.

He scoffs. "She doesn't hate you, she's in shock. And she's probably suspicious of you, but that'll fade with time, once she gets to know you."

"Why?" My face pinches, lips curling. "Why would she be suspicious of me?"

"She's protective of me. And of the family's money. But you don't have to worry about any of this, Mari. She'd be the same way if you were America's Sweetheart or the daughter of a sitting US president." He tugs his damp t-shirt off his body, revealing a glistening six-pack complete with two muscled arrows pointing to his ... family jewels. "But don't concern yourself with any of that. Just be yourself and leave the rest to me. By the way, you handled yourself well. Not that I'm surprised."

He strides down the hall toward his suite, and I follow because I'm not finished with this conversation.

"Is she going to be like this all summer?" I ask.

"Why? Does that change things?"

"Maybe."

He arches a dark brow. "Trust me, she'll get over it soon enough. Besides, with all the friends and family shuffling in and out all summer, she'll put on a good face. As for whether or not she truly likes you, well, I don't see how that should matter given the circumstances. And you really need to get over giving a fuck about whether people like you or not, Mari."

"I'm not used to people taking one look at me and deciding they don't like me. We don't do that where I come from."

He tugs at the string around his gym shorts, waiting for me to leave so he can get in the shower, but I'm still not through.

"Look, I don't want to sit here and go in circles with you, Maribel. Believe me when I tell you that whether or not Helena Rutherford likes you is irrelevant. *I* like you. Even if you don't like me. I think you're a good person. A smart person. A beautiful person. And I appreciate the sacrifice you're making for me. I'm asking a lot of you, and it's not lost on me." He glances over my shoulder and toward the doorway.

I'm quiet, soaking in what are possibly the nicest words this man has ever uttered to me.

"All right, fine. It's just that, if we were a real couple, I would never respect a man who couldn't stand up to his mother. If we were really in love and you let that go? I don't know if I'd be able to stay with you," I say.

"Did she offend you in some way? I don't see what all this fuss is about." His fingers trail beneath the waistband of his shorts, stopping. "Did I miss something or are you making this into a thing because you're anxious about how this is going to play out?"

"She was cold," I say. "And she stopped by for a visit, supposedly, but she couldn't get out of here fast enough. It was just odd to me."

"Should I have asked her to stay?" He lifts a

brow. "You seemed uncomfortable, Mari. Like you needed as much breathing room as she did."

"No." I pull my bottom lip between my thumb and forefinger, exhaling. "I don't know. The whole thing left me feeling unsettled. She was polite and all … but I don't know … I don't know."

"You keep saying that," he chuckles. "You're nervous. Don't be. Let me do the worrying. You just need to smile and nod and act like you're crazy about me."

My mouth tips up at the corner. Months of waiting on this man hand and foot contradict the way he wants to take me under his wings and bear my burdens. Maybe he's not such an asshole after all? I could get used to this redeeming side of him.

"Trust me. I intend to stand my ground this summer. You will be my number one. I'll ensure you're comfortable in everyone's presence, and I'll personally see to it that you're treated as one of the family," he says, moving toward me. He places his hands on my shoulders and exhales, and I drag in a lungful of his pheromone-laced masculine scent. "All you have to do is convince them you're in love with me. Everything else is in my hands. Can you do that for me? Can you leave the rest to me?"

Swallowing the nervous lump in my throat, I

nod, exhaling my Hudson-scented breath, and then I show myself out.

"Oh, and Maribel?" he calls seconds before I close his door.

"Yes?" I peek back in.

"Find us a flight to Omaha today, will you? I'd like to leave as soon as possible."

"Omaha?"

"Yes. You're from Orchard Hill, Nebraska correct? That's just outside of Omaha from what I understand," he says. "This morning's incident has me thinking that I'd like to meet your parents sooner rather than later."

Chapter Eleven

Hudson

"It's so …" I glance out the window as our plane makes its descent. Checking for the airport, I don't see it yet. I only see a whole lot of … nothing.

"Farm-y?" Mari finishes my sentence.

"I was going to say flat, but farm-y works."

The plane begins to shake and dip, every move exaggerated by the impossibly small size of this plane. Mari tightens her lap belt and grips the handles of her seat, closing her eyes. I tilt my head from side to side, stretching my strained neck. I can't remember the last time I flew coach, and I can't recall if I've ever flown on a plane this small that wasn't headed toward some tropical island paradise destination, but alas, this was all they had coming out of JFK to Omaha.

"You okay?" I ask as the plane pushes through another bout of turbulence. The door to the lavatory swings open, hitting the wall, and a flight attendant rushes to secure it. I feel the urge to reach for her hand because she really seems to be in distress, but I don't know if that would make things worse.

Mari nods as the plane drops in altitude. "I'm fine. This turbulence is … making me sick to my stomach."

The captain's voice comes over the speakers, telling us it's a balmy seventy-two degrees over Omaha right now and we'll be landing in approximately seven minutes.

"Here." I reach for the airsickness bag and hand it to her, but she waves it away.

"I'll be fine," she says.

"You're yellow. I've never seen a yellow person before." I half chuckle.

Without saying a word, she yanks the bag from my hand and covers her nose and mouth, squeezing her eyes tight. The plane drops once more and Mari empties her pretzel-filled stomach with one sickening retch.

***

I check the time on my phone as Mari comes out of the women's restroom just outside our terminal. Her hair is combed, her lips are slicked in balm, and the faint scent of mint trails from her lips.

"Feeling better now?" I ask.

Her hand rests on her lower stomach and she nods.

"Let's grab our luggage. Did you order a car service for us?" I ask.

"My parents are picking us up."

"Wait, what?"

"They insisted. My dad's a great driver. You won't even notice he's not wearing a suit or driving a limo." She fights a smirk.

"Smart ass."

We follow the signs to the baggage claim, arriving just in time to see our luggage pass by. Lunging simultaneously, we nearly knock each other over before turning to see a woman with bushy gray-blonde hair trotting in our direction with open arms.

"Mari!" the woman shrieks, happy. She wraps her arms around Mari and squeezes her tight, her matching blue eyes brimming with tears. "It's so good to see you. Look at you! You look great! We've missed you so much. Come on, your father's parked in the pick up lane. I told him not to, but you know how he is. Man won't listen to save his life." After a second, her smile fades and she turns her attention to me, seemingly unsure if I'm with them or simply following them.

"Mom, this is Hudson," Mari says. "Hudson, this is my mom, Margo."

Margo stares in my direction, taking me in like she's never seen a big-citied suit before.

"Mari, you said you were bringing a surprise, but I didn't know you meant you were bringing home a boyfriend." Margo's thin red lips spread into a smile as her expression lightens. Before I realize what's happening, she's wrapped her arms around me, her face pressed against my jacket. "He's so handsome, Mar. And he smells good too!"

I chuckle. I'd hug her back, but she's got my arms pinned to my sides.

"Thank you," I say when she lets me go.

"Actually, Mom. He's not my boyfriend— we're engaged." Mari winces, half-covering her pretty lips with a nervous hand.

"You're what?" Her mom's careful stare navigates between us.

"We're getting married." Mari flashes her eight carat engagement ring, her mouth inching up at the sides.

Margo grabs her hand, bringing the ring close to inspect it. "Is this real?"

Mari nods.

"Good, God." Margo lets her daughter's hand fall and steps back. "That's, um, beautiful. Wow. I'm ... speechless."

Mari turns to me. "For the record, my mom is almost never speechless, so ..."

"Shall we head to the car?" I ask. "If the airport security here is anything like New York, he's probably seconds from getting a ticket."

Margo laughs. "Oh, sweetheart. Nothing out here is anything like New York."

***

I'm seated behind Abel in the backseat of a quad cab Ford pick up. Every chance he gets, he checks his rearview, though I suspect he's looking at me. So far he seems nice. A bit quiet, but nice. Certainly not the shotgun wielding, threat-spewing small town father I'd conjured up in my head.

"So Hudson, where are you from originally?" Margo calls from the front seat. Abel's window is down and the truck's noise nearly prevents me from hearing my own thoughts.

"I was born in Manhattan, attended school mostly in Connecticut. At least until college," I answer.

"Where did you attend college?" she asks.

"NYU," I answer.

"Dad, it's super loud back here. Can you roll your window up?" Mari holds her hair back, keeping it from whipping around in her face.

A moment later it's quieter, but it's an awkward sort of quiet. I almost preferred the chaotic road noise.

"We should be home in about twenty minutes," Margo announces, not that anyone asked.

Abel reaches for the radio, tuning to a

country station and cranking up the most depressing song I've ever heard. Pulling in a deep breath, I glance out the window and take in the sights of the flattest terrain I've ever seen. Couldn't they have at least had the decency to plant a few extra trees out here? There's nothing to look at. Nothing.

Except Mari.

Subtly turning my attention to my affianced, I let my eyes follow the curves of her body, head to toe. Her soft blonde hair. Her full, rose-colored lips. Her crossed legs and the way her hand is slipped between them as she leans her head against the glass.

She must feel me watching her because out of nowhere she straightens her posture, whips toward me, and mouths, "What?"

"Nothing," I mouth back.

"Stop staring," she mouths.

"I'm not."

Fighting a smirk, she rolls her eyes, but not before letting them linger for a few seconds more.

***

"Hudson, I just have to apologize." Margo clutches her hands over her heart as we stand in the foyer of a 1970s-era split level. The exterior is painted cream with baby blue shutters and a soaring oak tree that's likely been there for decades. A basketball hoop is affixed over the two-car garage and a parked, tarp-covered car takes up one of the spots. "We had no idea you were coming, so the bed situation is a little ... well, Abel's been sleeping on the sofa because he threw his back out last week. And we turned the guest room into a man cave just after Christmas. You'll have to stay with Mari in her room."

"That's fine," I say. "No need to apologize."

"It's a double bed." Margo winces. "It'll be tight."

"It's just two nights. We'll be fine," Mari says. "Hudson loves to cuddle anyway. Don't you?"

She winks in my direction.

"You know me well," I say.

Abel glances at me through the corner of his eye. I'm sure the idea of some strange man sleeping in his daughter's bed with her doesn't exactly appeal to him, but it is what it is. I'd offer to stay at a hotel, but I don't want to insult them.

Hoisting our luggage up half a staircase, we turn to the left and head down a bedroom hall.

"Mari's room is the last one on the left." Margo points. "Bathroom is over here on the right. We all share one and the lock is broken, so just knock before you go in. I'm going to get supper started, so feel free to make yourself at home while you wait."

Her mother leaves, and we head into a small bedroom painted in a sunny shade of yellow with a small double bed anchoring a wall covered in posters and photographs. In the corner rests a mountain of stuffed animals, many of which have clearly seen better days, and a rainbow lamp is nestled on a scratched white nightstand.

"I can't believe you're in my childhood bedroom." Mari plops down on the edge of the bed, her hands sliding across the floral comforter.

"This room looks like the early two-thousands had a baby and that baby threw up all over." I move closer to inspect the collage wall. "Backstreet Boys, Mari? Seriously? Ninety-Eight Degrees?"

"I had a boy band phase. So what?"

I take a seat beside her. "It smells like … fruit … in here."

"That'd be Mr. Strawberry." She points to the corner. "My stuffed bear. Still smells like a dream after all these years."

"Mr. Strawberry? What an original name."

"Eight-year-old me takes offense to that."

"Eight-year-old you should be offended. That's an atrocious name for a bear."

"He smells like strawberries and came with a strawberry on his t-shirt. It made sense," she says, shrugging.

"If we ever have fake babies to go with this fake marriage, remind me not to let you name them," I tease.

"Fake babies weren't part of the contract," she says, tutting her finger. "If you want the privilege of breeding with me, it'll cost you."

"Breeding with you? What are you, a dog?"

"I have good genes, Hudson. You saw my parents. Mom's in her late forties and sometimes she gets carded when she tries to buy margaritas at Los Charros." Mari shrugs again.

"Anyway. All this talk about genes and babies is making me lose my appetite. Where should I hang my clothes for the weekend?" I rise from the bed, scanning the small room and heading toward her closet. "Is there room in here?"

Mari flinches. "Probably not."

Yanking the doors open, I'm met with a wall of clothes upon clothes, all crammed in so tight I doubt a man could fit a piece of paper between them.

"What is this? Every article of clothing you've ever owned?" I shake my head.

She rises, closing the doors. "I was an only child. And my parents liked to spoil me. I couldn't throw them out. They worked hard to be able to buy those for me."

"So you're just going to keep them forever?" I ask.

"I don't know. I haven't really thought about when I'm going to throw them out. Honestly, I was waiting for one of them to suggest it, but no one's said anything, so they're just hanging out in the closet for now." Mari points to the dresser. "You can use the bottom two drawers. They should be empty."

"What are you going to use then?"

"I'll just keep everything in my suitcase. Not a big deal." She watches as I place my suitcase on her bed and begin unloading. "Do you really need all that stuff for two days?"

"I hate being unprepared," I say. "That's why I have Marta overpack."

Mari takes a seat on the side of the bed, her leg bent underneath her. "Speaking of Marta ... when you told her what we were doing, did she act weird about it?"

I glance to the left. "No. Not at all. Why?"

"No reason."

"Did she say something to you?"

"Of course not."

"Then why are you asking?" I ask.

"It's nothing. I was just curious if she was on board or not with this," she says. I call bullshit.

"Does it matter what Marta thinks?" I ask. "She's my employee. I'm sure she has a lot of opinions about me, but it's her job to keep them to herself. You let me know if she's ever conducting herself in an unprofessional manner."

"Marta is great." Mari forces a smile. "Anyway, dinner's probably going to be ready soon. We stay in here much longer they're going to think we're messing around, and then dinner's going to be just as awkward as the ride home was."

"It wasn't awkward."

"It was so awkward. I don't think my dad knows what to make of it all. Can't say I blame him." Mari moves toward the door, her hand clutched around the knob. "Come on. We can't hide in here the whole weekend. Let's show them how over-the-moon in love we are. Babe."

I smirk, making my way to her. I'm loving this playful side of her and whatever it is she's bringing out in me. In a weird way, while I've orchestrated this entire situation, it kind of feels like it's us against the world.

We have this secret, she and I. And the trust between us, while it's still sort of gelling, it's actually kind of hot.

Slipping my hand around hers, I lead her down the hall toward her mother's kitchen, which smells of frying ground beef and fresh vegetables. Halfway, I stop to admire the childhood school pictures that line the hall in grade-order. As a kindergartener, Mari had a chubby face and a smattering of light freckles that have since faded. In first grade, her front two teeth were missing, but it didn't keep her from smiling her heart out. From the looks of her second grade picture, she must have attempted an at-home perm.

"Stop." Mari yanks on my hand. "Come on."

"You were a cute kid," I say.

She turns to me, her eyes smiling. "See, you already have something in common with my parents. They were convinced I was the cutest kid ever to walk the face of the earth. They even got me a talent agent. They were convinced I was going to be the next Hilary Duff."

"How'd that work out for you?"

"I was in a JC Penney catalog. Once."

"Adorable," I say as she pulls me into the kitchen. My stomach rumbles as I breathe in another whiff of her mother's cooking. I can't remember the last time I enjoyed home-style fare.

"There they are," Margo announces over a sizzling pan on the stove. "Have a seat, guys. Food'll be done shortly."

I take a spot next to Abel, who's still looking me over with a blank expression on his face. I like to think I'm good at reading people, but this man is stone-like, unmoving.

"Dad," Mari says, grabbing his attention. "How are things at the shop? Staying busy?"

Margo brings a plate of biscuits and deposits them in the center of the oak table. Abel steals one, shoving half of it in his mouth.

"My dad owns a repair shop," Mari says. "He can restore just about anything. People are always bringing in their clocks and lawnmowers and weed-eaters and bread makers. Random things. Not much he can't fix."

"Is that so?" I ask, turning to Abel. "I've always believed some people were just born with a natural inclination to take things apart and put them back together the right way. There's some inherent curiosity in there, too, to see how things work. I find those sorts of things fascinating myself. I love to look at things from a very basic level, all their parts and pieces, and fit them together."

"Hudson, what do you do for a living?" Margo calls from the kitchen.

"I'm an architect," I say.

Abel's eyes move from me to his daughter, and he points as he chews. "Weren't you working for some asshole architect in the city? This isn't him, is it?"

I watch the color drain from Mari's face.

"No, no," she says, her tone almost frantic. "This isn't him. This is a different architect. We met at a … work thing … I was there. And he was there. And we met."

"Good," Abel says with a huff. "If you brought that jerk here, I'd be kicking him to the curb."

"Dad." Mari tilts her head, releasing a nervous chuckle. "I've been ranting and raving about how nice we are here in Nebraska. Don't make a liar out of me."

"Here we are," Margo interrupts, bringing over a skillet of what appears to be noodles and hamburger drowning in some kind of cheesy sauce. "I hope cheeseburger pasta's okay with you, Hudson? You don't have any allergies, do you?"

"None," I say, placing a paper napkin over my lap. "Smells wonderful, Mrs. Collins."

"Please, call me Margo," she says. "Dig in. I can't wait to hear more about how you two lovebirds met!"

Mari and I exchange looks.

"You want to tell them?" I ask her.

"Maybe you should?" She bats her lashes, resting her chin on the top of her hands. "You tell the story so well."

Chuffing, I smirk as I dish up a couple ladles of cheeseburger pasta. "Okay, well, it was a snowy day in January. I was headed to an architectural conference at this hotel on the Lower East Side. I walked in, dusted the snow off my jacket, and glanced around to get my bearings. Only I found myself distracted by this blonde woman holding an armful of blueprint tubes as she chased after her boss, who clearly didn't appreciate her hard work — I could tell that just by looking at the schmuck," I add. "Anyway, I watched her. I was captivated, really. She carried herself with such poise and grace. I saw her chatting with someone she knew, maybe another co-worker? I'm not sure. Anyway, she smiled, and I was a goner."

I place my hand over my chest.

"I knew then and there that I had to meet her," I say. "I had to get to know her. I wanted that beautiful smile of hers all to myself. So I introduced myself."

Abel watches me, unmoving, and Margo is clearly entranced by my story.

Reaching my hand across the table, I place it over Mari's.

"When the moment was right, I approached her," I say. "I told her my name. Asked hers. She wasn't interested. Not at first. It wasn't easy. I can't say it was love at first sight, at least not on her end. But we talked a bit more, and we were able to find some common ground. After that, we began spending time together. And now here we are."

"Tell us how you popped the question!" Margo bats her hand at me, giddy and giggling.

"We were wandering Fifth Avenue one afternoon, after an amazing lunch at our favorite restaurant, and we stopped in front of a Cartier store. There was a display in the window that caught her eye, and I don't know what came over me, but I decided right then and there to ask her to marry me," I say.

"I told him he was insane," Mari interjects. "And then he dragged me inside and forced me to pick out the most beautiful ring I'd seen in my life."

"True story." I squeeze her hand. "Anyway, I had to lock this one down before she got away.

She's special, this woman. Knew that from the moment I saw her."

Margo dabs at her eyes, and Abel's expression softens for the first time all afternoon.

"Well, can we just say, we're so excited to get to know you, Hudson," Margo says. "It's absolutely wonderful seeing our daughter so in love, and maybe things are happening a little fast, but I want you to know that we're thrilled to have you join our family."

Margo pushes her chair out from the table, coming around and giving me another bear hug.

"Thank you," I say.

Abel clears his throat. "Yes. Welcome to the family. Congratulations, you two."

"When's the wedding?" Margo asks.

Mari glances my way, lifting her brows as if she, too, is curious.

"We're still settling on a date," I say, bringing her hand to my lips and pressing a kiss into her soft skin. "But the sooner the better."

Chapter Eleven

Mari

"Who knew Hudson Rutherford could be so charming?" I ask, keeping my voice low, as he slips into my room that night. I'm already in pajamas, an old t-shirt and sweats, and making myself comfortable on my half of the double bed. He's just returned from washing up.

"What are you talking about?" he smirks, flicking out the light.

After Hudson spun the tale of our whirlwind romance to my parents, he then proceeded to gush about how beautiful I was, inside and out, and how he plans to spend the rest of his days seeing to it that I'm well cared for.

"My mom thinks you're the most amazing thing ever," I say, "and my dad has completely warmed up to you. He doesn't show just anyone his fancy power tools, you know. Only the special ones."

"Oh, yeah?" He flips the covers back on his side before climbing in.

"It's great and all that you've convinced my parents that you're crazy about me," I say, "but what's going to happen when we go our separate ways? They're going to be crushed. I don't like this. I don't like lying to them."

He turns on his side, resting his head on his hands. His forehead is covered in lines as he exhales.

"I'm sorry," he says. "I'm sorry that this is the way it has to be. I don't like it either, but would you rather have them in on the lie? Would you rather force them to lie for you?"

"I'd rather not involve them at all." I sigh, sinking into the covers. "Anyway, it's too late to turn back now. I just ... I don't know. Watching them tonight and seeing how big their smiles were and how enchanted they were with everything you were saying ... I guess when I agreed to this, I didn't think about how it would affect them."

"I meant what I said," he says. "I'm going to see to it that you're cared for for the rest of your life. That money will go far for you if you invest it wisely, and I'll see to it that you're set up with the best financial planners in the industry. And once we go our separate ways, just say we got caught up, we rushed things, and we amicably decided to end it. That's all. They'll understand."

Rolling to my side, I face him, looking into his deep blues. "Must be rough always having all the answers."

"I like a good puzzle, a good challenge."

"You like taking things apart and putting them back together," I say, remembering what he said earlier at dinner.

"I do."

"And here I just thought you liked to design things."

"It's sort of the same thing," he says.

I watch him, bathed in the glow of moonlight that spills in from my bedroom window. This moment is completely surreal. My jerk boss, lying in my childhood bed, moments from drifting off beside me.

"If you could take me apart, how would you fix me?" I ask, eyelashes slightly fluttery as my body begins to shut down for the night like one of those old desktop computers that take forever. I'm fighting the spinning wheel.

"It's been a long day, Mari."

"Before we go to sleep, can you just answer that?" I ask. "Or is that what you did with the makeover and the ring and all that. Was that your way of fixing me up?"

"Not at all," I say. "Those things were costumes. Props. Mari, you don't need fixing. Now go to sleep."

I feel my lips pull into a sleepy grin as I roll over. We're not touching, but I can feel his body heat, and when his breathing slows, I know he's already out.

His kind words replay in my head just as I float off.

Maybe … just maybe … he's not such a jerk after all.

***

The sweet chirping of birds outside my window at dawn wakes me the next morning, only when I roll over, I find the other half of the bed cold and empty. Sitting up, I rub my eyes before taking a look around.

Flinging the covers off, I tiptoe out of bed and head down the hall to where my mother is singing some Fleetwood Mac song at the top of her lungs as she fries bacon in a skillet.

"Where's Hudson?" I ask, startling her.

She whips around, her hand pressed over her heart as she laughs. "Good morning, sweetheart. He's in the garage with your father. They're tinkering around with … something. I don't know."

She swats her hand through the air then turns back around to tend to the cooking, and I glance at the clock. It's too early to be tinkering with anything. Plopping down at one of the old swivel bar stools at the peninsula, I watch my mom cook.

Just like old times.

Mom keeps singing, belting *Rhiannon* so loud I'm pretty sure the McKenzies on the corner can hear her, but I just smile.

"What do you think of him, Mom?" I ask while I have her alone.

She spins around. "Who? Hudson?"

I laugh, nodding. "Yeah. Who else?"

"I like him," she says. "He doesn't seem like a bullshitter to me. You know how much I hate bullshitters. You can tell he's very intelligent. Very hardworking. Your father respects that. You chose well, Maribel. We're shocked, but we're proud."

This moment is more bittersweet than I thought it would be. Someday, when I'm really engaged and truly in love, someday when I tell my parents I'm actually getting married—for real—it'll be for the second time. And they might hold back then. They might not take me seriously. Or they might not want to get their hopes up.

There'll never be another first time.

"Why don't you go tell them it's time to eat?" Mom plates the bacon before cracking an egg over a bowl. "I'm sure they're starving; they've been out there for an hour."

"An hour?" Where the hell have I been?

I head for the garage, opening the heavy wooden door before lingering at the screen door, watching the two of them as they're huddled over my father's workbench. Hudson has a pencil in his fingers and he's pointing. My father nods, eyebrows lifted. I can't hear them over my dad's oldies-blasting radio, but they seem to be deep in discussion.

Stepping past the door, I clear my throat, commanding their attention.

"Hey, angel," my dad says.

"Hi," Hudson's eyes meet mine.

"What are you doing?" I ask.

"Hudson's trying to help me with this shed I want to build out back. He says he can design one that matches our house. Like a miniature version. Your mother always says she doesn't want one of those kit sheds that stick out like a sore thumb." Dad smiles when he looks at Hudson. Somehow, in under twenty-four hours, Hudson has managed to melt my father's carefully reserved demeanor ... which is completely insane considering everything I know about this man.

"Mom says breakfast is ready," I say, heading back in with a heavy heart.

It's one thing for Hudson to charm my parents, to convince them he's in love with me.

It's something else entirely to make promises he doesn't intend on keeping. I highly doubt he's going to be drafting up shed plans the second we're back in New York, not with his backlist of high profile, big-moneyed clients waiting impatiently for their turn with one of the most sought-after architects in all of Manhattan.

Turning on my heel, I head back in, letting the screen door slam behind me.

Chapter Twelve

Hudson

"You okay?" I find Mari on the front steps of the house after dinner that night. "You've been quiet all day."

She glances up. "Between you and my parents, I can't really get a word in edgewise."

I chuckle. "You say that like it's a bad thing. Your parents love me. You should be happy."

"It's fine that they like you, Hudson, but promising to design my father's shed? Promising my mother you'll send her tickets to Hamilton?" She turns away. "You don't have to buy their affections. And you certainly don't have to weasel your way into their hearts with gifts and promises."

I take the spot beside her, the concrete cool and gravel-pocked beneath my hands.

"I don't understand what all of this is about, Mari. Everything's going well," I say, watching her from my periphery.

"Too well."

"So …?"

"Don't hurt them," she says. "Keep your promises. All of them."

I laugh. "That's all this is? You don't think I'll keep my word?"

"You're not exactly known for being kind and generous," she says. "At least not since I've known you. Kind of makes me feel like this whole thing is disingenuous." She places her hand out. "I mean, I know *this* is pretend. But my parents? They're real people with real feelings."

I take her hand in mine. "It's sweet the way you worry about them. But I can assure you, Mari, I have every intention of keeping my promises to them. You don't have to worry."

"And if you don't?" she asks.

"I *will*."

She inhales, releasing it slowly as she peers toward the sunset as it falls beneath a playground in the distance.

"I need a walk," she announces. "You want to take one?"

Mari rises, dusting off her hands.

"You're barefoot," I say.

"It's been a long time since I've been able to roam the streets barefoot." A slow smile curls her lips. "You should try it."

"The concrete will tear up the soles of your feet."

Mari shrugs. "It feels *so* good though. Just try it. Trust me."

I hesitate and she drops to her knees, pulling at my laces and forcing my shoes off. When she's done, she tosses them in the grass.

"Come on, city boy." She tugs on my arm and I follow her down the driveway to a broken sidewalk laced with weed-filled cracks juxtaposed with lush, green lawns that have been tended for decades.

"Is this the kind of thing you do for fun in Orchard Hill?" I tease.

"Don't make fun. It's not polite." She nudges me as we pad along the concrete. I won't admit it, but it does feel nice … if only in a strange way. It's almost … freeing. "So what else do you do around here?"

"Um." She swings her arms, taking long, slow strides. "We usually just hang out with each other. Friends, family. Most of my extended family still lives around here. My grandparents and two aunts and one uncle all live in, like, a five-block radius."

"You're joking."

"Nope." She glances at me, smiling. "Do you think that's weird?"

"Not weird. Just different," I say.

"I never realized how different Orchard Hill was until I left," she muses. "Nobody locks their doors around here. You could probably walk into just about any house you wanted."

"That's insane."

"I know! But there's hardly any crime. Everyone knows everyone. It's just a more trusting community, I guess? Now, knowing what I know and having lived in the city for a few years, I would never. But that's how it is here. It's the norm."

We turn the corner, climbing a small hill surrounded by mid-century modern homes and quaint little ranches. In the distance appears to be a block of estate-type homes: Victorians, European Romantics, and turn-of-the-century Queen Annes.

142

I'm sure back in the day, those housed the town's doctors and lawyers. I can only hope their current owners have restored them to their former glory.

"Where'd you grow up? You told my parents you were born in Manhattan, but is that where you were raised?" she asks.

I pause. "I attended boarding school in Connecticut from kindergarten through eighth grade. In high school, my parents sent me to a prep school—which was just another boarding school. Headed to college after that. I'm not sure that I was really raised by anyone other than teachers and school administrators."

"Oh. I'm sorry." She pouts and we mull in our respective silences. "Sucks you didn't have a traditional childhood."

"Yes," I say with a bittersweet chuff. "It does ... suck."

"Must have been awful," she says softly, "being sent away as a child and not understanding why."

"My parents always said it was in my best interest. It was for my future. They were doing it for me." I shake my head. "They weren't doing it for anyone but themselves. They wanted to be able to go yachting in the Maldives and skiing in the French Alps at a moment's notice. A child would've made their life … complicated. It was easier to send me away, where I would have round-the-clock supervision, three square meals, a world-class education, and plenty of socialization."

"That's what they told you?"

"We always had our summers in Montauk. That was our family time."

"That's all you got from them? A few months of the year and then they shipped you off again?"

"Yeah."

"That's terrible," she says, exhaling. "Sorry. I don't mean to judge your parents."

"Don't worry about it. I've judged them my whole life." I huff. "They are who they are. There's no changing them. There's no taking back what they did."

"Is that why you pour yourself into your work?" she asks.

I glance ahead. We're getting closer to the street with the antique houses. They're all I can think about. I don't want to discuss my childhood anymore. I don't want to talk about—or think about—the fact that I may or may not have abandonment issues as a result of never truly feeling wanted by my parents.

It's neither here nor there. Truly.

"See that white house?" I point north. "It has a triangular pediment set against a hipped roof with dormers. It's a Queen Anne."

"Oh," she says. "We always called that the Pauley House. It's haunted. Or that's what everyone says. Some kids died there in the 1920s. Drowned in the pool when the nanny was supposed to be watching them. So sad."

"How tragic."

"What about that stone house? I always thought it looked like a castle," she says. "When I was a little girl, I'd ride my bike up and down this street and pretend that I was a princess and that was my house."

"That's a European Romantic," I say. "You can tell by the asymmetric composition and the half-timbered accents. The light stone is fairly typical too. Sometimes you'll see stucco."

Warm drops of rain begin to pepper the sidewalk, dampening our clothes in the process. A

145

clap of thunder groans in the distance. Spring is nothing if not a temperamental woman: loving on you one minute, chasing you off the next.

Without saying a word, we turn back, leaving the picturesque street in the distance, and by the time we're halfway home, the rain picks up and begins to pour. Rustling leaves in the ancient oaks above us do little to protect us, and by the time we reach the front door, we're both soaked.

Standing in the foyer, we lock eyes. Mari laughs, her hair sticking to her cheeks and neck, and rainwater pools at our bare feet. My shoes are in the yard, but I'm not concerned with them right now.

I can't stop looking at her, all wet and vulnerable.

This may be a fake relationship, but this woman is as real as they come.

My eyes fall on her lips, my hands aching to reach for her chin and angle it just so.

"I'm going to go change," she says, as if she picked up on my intentions.

Dashing up the stairs, she disappears around the corner.

Chapter Thirteen

Mari

"Mari?" Hudson creeps into my darkened room. I hear him changing out of his damp clothes and slipping into something dry, and then I feel the dip of the mattress when he takes a spot next to me.

I don't know what happened.

Everything was going well until we stood in the foyer, rain-soaked and eyes holding steady. Something told me he was about to kiss me, and I couldn't let that happen, so I bolted.

I hid.

I tucked myself away in my room, under the covers, nose buried in a book on my phone.

"You just left me. I thought you were coming back," he says. "You okay?"

No.

No, I'm not okay because part of me wanted

to kiss him too. And part of me is starting to like him ... not romantically, but as a human being.

This entire arrangement was a hell of a lot easier when I hated him with the fury of a million Flaming Hot Cheetos.

"Sorry. I needed to lie down," I say. "Didn't mean to leave you hanging."

"It's okay. Your dad wanted to run some more shed ideas past me," he climbs under the covers.

It's dark now, thanks in part to the storm rolling through. The windows rattle, pelted by a spray of rain every odd second.

"You wanted to kiss me earlier, didn't you?" I ask. If I don't come out and say this, it's going to be on my mind all night, keeping me up, and we're supposed to catch an early flight home in the morning.

"What?"

"You heard me." I sit up, turning toward him.

"Is that why you ran off? Because you thought I was going to kiss you?" he asks.

"I didn't think. I knew. I could sense it." I visually trace the outline of his body in the dark, under the random illumination of lightning flashes. He's handsome in a way I never wanted to fully accept. He's chiseled. And beautiful. Long dark lashes. Dimpled chin. Deep-as-the-ocean blue eyes. Thick hair I could run my fingers through. A body built for sin. The list goes on.

"You're going to have to kiss me sooner or later," he says. "Unless you want our first kiss to be on our wedding day."

I inhale, letting it go a few seconds later. The words are terrifying, but they're right there, on the tip of my tongue, and I have to say them.

"I don't want this to get so complicated that we don't know where fake ends and real begins," I blurt.

"Mari, I don't want to be married. I don't do monogamy or commitment. If I kiss you … if I touch you … it'll be because I think you're gorgeous and sexy and you turn me on. It won't be because I'm in love with you and want to spend the rest of my life with you. You don't need to worry about any of this becoming real. It might be *really* fun, but it won't be real love. I can promise you that."

His brutal honesty stings, despite the fact that he's saying the words I needed to hear.

"I don't do the no-strings things," I say.

"Have you done it before?"

"Yeah. And it didn't end so well for me."

"What happened?" he asks.

"I'd rather not say."

"Let me guess," Hudson says. "You wanted no-strings, ended up falling for the guy thinking you'd be the one to change him, and he left you high and dry?"

"Nope."

"Then what happened?"

"I *said* I don't want to talk about it."

He reaches for my cheek, causing me to flinch at his touch. Just weeks ago, the sight of this man used to put my stomach in knots with anxiety, and now he's in my bed, touching me like I'm some kind of porcelain doll, the object of his affection.

"I won't kiss you if you don't want me to," he says. "But I'm just saying … you might actually enjoy it."

"I doubt that."

"Hell bent on convincing yourself you still hate me?" he asks.

"I don't hate you, Hudson."

"I know you don't. But you wish you did," he says.

"You're right." I can't argue with him. He hit the nail on the head. Rolling to my back, I pull the covers up and sink into the pillow, staring at the ceiling and the crooked ceiling fan that wobbles with each spin. "You're absolutely right."

Chapter Fourteen

Hudson

"New girl, what's your name again?" I ask the mousey brunette seated at Mari's old desk Monday morning. The temp agency sent her after I requested their best. This has to be some kind of fucking joke. The girl's shaking like a leaf, sitting with her arms clenched at her sides like she's afraid to touch anything.

"Shoshannah," she says, her voice as meek as that pathetic aura she's giving off. A few months working with me and she'll find her spine, I'm sure of it.

"All right, Savannah, I like my coffee by eight fifteen, and when my office door is closed, that means you are to pretend I don't exist." I grab a stack of mail off the corner of her desk. "If you need anything, ask one of the girls down the hall."

"Sure. Yes. Okay," she says, nodding quickly. "And it's Shoshannah."

"That's what I said." I turn and head to my office, trying not to chuckle. Breaking in the new ones never fails to amuse me.

Once in my office, I fire up my computer and pull up my CAD program. I've got a backlog of projects, but I promised Abel I'd whip him up the backyard shed of his dreams, so that's what I'm going to do.

I'm working on the gable roof when my phone rings.

"Yes, Savannah?" I answer.

"I-it's Sh-shoshannah," she corrects me again, stumbling over her words. I must terrify her already. "You have a call on line two."

"Who is it?" I ask, frowning.

"I-I didn't ask. I'm sorry."

"Always ask, Savannah." I hang up and press line two. "This is Hudson."

"Are you being nice?" a woman's voice comes through from the other end.

"I beg your pardon?"

"You said the new girl was starting today. I'm just calling to make sure you're being nice."

"Hi, Mari." I smirk. Smart ass. "Did you need something or were you calling to impart your sage advice?"

"The world is already full of assholes. Why be one more?"

"I don't have time to rehash a stale conversation."

"I just remember how my first day was," she says with a hopeless sigh. "God, you were an ass. And I love that I can tell you that now. Don't think for one second I'll ever let you live it down."

"I wouldn't dream of it."

"What's the new girl's name?" she asks.

"Shoshanna."

"Is that her name or is that just what you're calling her?"

I chuff. "Don't you have something else to tend to? I don't have time for … pointless chit chat."

"Actually, no. I have nothing to do because you keep me holed up in your tower like some princess, some canary in a gilded cage," she says.

"Do you know how many women would kill

to be a canary in my cage?"

"I'm sure there's a plethora of women, Hudson. I'm sure they're lined up the block and around the corner," she says. "But being a kept woman isn't my thing, and I'm bored out of my freaking mind here."

"Take a pottery class. My treat."

"Pottery?"

"Yoga?"

"Nah," she says. "I'm not that flexible."

"That's a shame. Go get your nails done. Go shopping. Catch a show on Broadway. My treat. Just … find something to do," I say, sighing as I click my mouse.

"Fine. I'll take Isabelle out for lunch," she says. "What are you working on? I can hear you clicking around."

"Your father's tool shed."

"No shit?" She laughs.

"Goodbye, Mari. I'll see you this evening." Hanging up, I shake my head, finding myself fighting off the amusement tickling my ribs. This woman makes me smile. And laugh. And I don't quite know how I feel about it yet.

I wasn't expecting to enjoy her company to this extent.

I wasn't expecting to enjoy my time in Orchard Hill, Nebraska or to sleep like a baby in that tiny double bed, my body pressed against hers.

And I sure as hell wasn't expecting to miss her (and her smart mouth) when she's not around.

My phone buzzes on the corner of my desk.

SIENNA: Back from Paris! Going to be in town this wknd. Want to hook up?

ME: Busy. Sorry.

SIENNA: Seriously?

SIENNA: …

SIENNA: Hudson?

SIENNA: Whatever. Your loss.

SIENNA: You're lucky you have a big dick. That's the only remotely likeable quality about you. Asshole.

A month ago I would have jumped at the chance to have a night with Sienna. Out of all the girls whose numbers fill my phone, she was always my number one. I would rearrange my entire schedule for an evening with the woman whose sexual stamina nearly outrivaled mine.

But times have changed.

I'm a taken man now … if only for the next few months.

I wait for Sienna to calm down and quit blowing up my phone, and then I power it down. A morning full of interruptions is no way to start a productive Monday, and I've got way too much shit to take care of.

Finishing up Abel's shed, I save the file and email the blueprints to the address Abel scribbled down for me on a scrap of paper last weekend.

I haven't told Mari yet, but Abel pulled me aside before we left and made me promise never to hurt her.

I gave him my word.

Chapter Fifteen

Mari

"Where's Marta?" Hudson removes his jacket as soon as he walks in the door tonight, draping it over his left arm as he makes his way to the kitchen.

"I gave her the night off." I stir the veggies I'm sautéing. "Thought I'd make us dinner."

"You didn't have to do that."

"This is what couples do. They cook for each other. This is all in the name of practice and authenticity."

His hands graze my sides, but only for a passing moment. If I didn't know better, I'd think he wanted to kiss me.

But he knows how I feel about that.

"Why don't you get comfortable and meet me in the dining room?" I ask, plating the food.

Candles are lit, music is playing, places are set, and the curtains are pulled to reveal a glowing, twilight city view.

This is about as romantic as it's ever going to get for us, but I'll take it.

A minute later, I meet him with the food, taking my seat to his right.

"I never knew you could cook," he says, reaching for his fork. I've poured him a glass of wine already, filling my glass with water. I figured if I did it ahead of time, it would save him from pointing out once again that I'm not drinking. "It smells wonderful."

"Thank you." I scoot closer, watching as he takes his first bite, then his second.

I never knew I could cook either, but with all this extra time on my hands, I was able to scour YouTube in search of some decent cooking videos, head to the organic grocery store on the corner, and head back in time to fix dinner before he got home.

"We're leaving for Montauk in a few days," he says a few minutes later.

"I thought we weren't going until the end of the month?"

"My mother called and wanted to move everything up. Apparently she's in full planning mode for our engagement party and there's a little beach club with a party room available this Saturday."

"That's nice of her to throw us a party." I fork a small broccoli spear. "She doesn't have to do that."

"Helena Rutherford will use any excuse she can find to throw a party. She lives for this."

"Do you always call your mother by her full name?" I chuckle.

He pauses. "Now that you mention it, I do tend to do that, don't I?"

I nod.

"I guess, growing up, she was never really just ... Mother ... she was always this larger-than-life commanding presence," he says. "She was simply ... Helena Rutherford."

"Or maybe calling her by her full name helped you to detach?" I shrug. "I'm sure part of you felt abandoned by her growing up."

"Anyway." He takes another bite before reaching for his wine glass and taking two swigs.

"So tell me about Montauk," I say. "Who's going to be there? What are we going to do? What's the house like? What can I expect?"

"My parents will be there, of course," he says. "And the Sheffields. Some aunts and uncles will drop in certain weekends. Maybe some cousins. Neighbor friends. There are constantly people coming and going. You'll never be bored. The house is a work of art that's been in the family for generations. You won't be disappointed."

"What do you do for fun there?"

"There are beaches. Magnificent restaurants. We sail. Water-ski. Listen to live music. Host cookouts. Go yachting. Parasailing. Horseback riding. Hold bonfires. You can do anything your little heart desires, Mari."

"How long are we staying, again?"

"Four weeks, give or take." He takes another sip before glancing out the window toward the city. The lack of sunshine casts dark shadows on the buildings, and street lights begin to flicker and glow. "It'll go by quickly though. It always does."

After we finish dinner, we take our dishes to the kitchen, and he places his next to the sink before walking off. I flick the water on and grab a bottle of dish soap from a lower cabinet, filling the stainless steel basin with soapy water.

"What are you doing?" he asks.

I lift a brow. "Cleaning up."

"Marta can handle it in the morning." He waves his hand, walking away, and without thinking, I reach for the sprayer nozzle and douse his back.

Hudson startles when the cold water hits him, spinning on his heel and barreling toward me.

"Oh, yeah? You want to play games?" he says, laughing and wrangling the sprayer out of my hands. Turning it toward me, he soaks my white blouse until very little is left to the imagination.

"What was that for?" I pretend to be pissed, but I'm actually digging this playful side of him.

"I was just getting you back."

"I sprayed you because you were acting like a spoiled brat." I glance at the water still streaming from the tap and then quickly cup my hands, filling them. Tossing a handful of warm water at his face, he ducks and it lands with a slick plop all over the marble tile floor.

Hudson does the same, only when I try to duck, I slip and fall on my ass, landing in a small puddle. He falls to his knees, coming toward me.

I'm giggling, breathless, completely in the moment as he gets closer, reaching his hands up my outer thighs and pulling me toward him. My hair sticks to my face and my shirt clings to my skin. I want to rip it off, I want to go change, but I also want to stay here. Right here. With him.

He's laughing. I'm laughing.

And before I know it, he's hovering over top of me. Our stares lock. Our smiles fade. I close my eyes only for a moment, and then I feel the rushed heat of his lips crushing mine, the slick of his velvet tongue, the unapologetic hardness between his hips as he grinds against me.

My hands reach for his face, sliding past his chiseled jaw and hooking at the nape of his neck, fingers tracing his drenched, dark hair.

I let him kiss me.

I don't ask him to stop.

I go with it, knowing full well it's probably not going to end well when this is all said and done, but it feels too good to quit.

His hips press harder against mine, the graze of his cock sending shivers through my body.

Hudson's hand tugs at the hem of my top, pulling it up until my damp skin is exposed to the cool air. My stomach caves at his touch, and a rush of blood floods my senses as his fingers travel higher, slipping beneath my bra.

His palm glides over my hardened buds, my chest rising and falling in quick succession.

I can't breathe.

And I kind of love it ...

He kisses me again, harder this time, and his free hand snakes down my right thigh, pulling it closer against his side as he grinds into me.

A rogue moan escapes my lips, my body and mind succumbing to this experience, my heart just along for the ride.

I want to tell myself that I can do this.

I've done one-night stands before.

I've had no-strings sex.

I've sought physical pleasure for the sake of a decent orgasm or two without so much as a second thought.

It's not a foreign concept to me.

Hudson sits back, his eyes poring over me before he rises to his feet. Leaning down, he helps me up. My body shakes and shivers. It's cold without his touch to keep me warm.

"Hudson, what are we—"

"Shh ..." He pulls me against him, his hands circling my waist as he kisses me again. His lips are soft, but his kisses are greedy, powerful.

Tugging my shirt over my head, he trails his fingers down my collarbone before pressing a kiss into my damp skin. Pulling the satin straps of my bra down my shoulders, he then unclasps the back, letting it fall to the floor and leaving me completely exposed.

"God, you're beautiful, Mari," he says, cupping the round fullness of my swollen breasts in his generous hands. It feels good to be touched like this, to be wanted and craved. Desired. "You have no fucking idea how badly I want you."

I bite my bottom lip to stifle a smile.

"This is coming from the man who, just a few weeks ago, berated me in front of an entire conference room of co-workers for getting his coffee order wrong," I say, voice soft.

"You did it on purpose."

"I know."

He squeezes my ass, pulling me closer before lifting me against him. My legs slide around his hips, grazing his hardness once more and sending a feverish gallop to my heart.

I know what comes next.

It would take an ungodly amount of self-restraint to put a stop to all of this, and unfortunately I'm only human.

I'm a horny, pregnant human.

Hudson carries me down the hall, to his suite, and deposits me in the center of his bed before yanking at his belt and unzipping his fly. He watches me as he works each button of his starched white shirt before pulling it off his shoulders. Sitting up, I reach for his waistband, tugging until his cock is free and his slacks fall at his feet.

The city lights shine through his naked windows, painting our bodies in shades of yellows and ambers.

Reaching for his stomach, my anxious fingers trace each ripple of his muscled wall.

We're doing this.

"Is this weird for you?" I ask as he drops to his knees and works my leggings down my thighs.

"Not at all," he says. "You?"

"Yeah."

He stops, glancing up at me with a wicked glint in his blue irises. "You want me to stop?"

"Nope," I say, lying on my back.

He peels my leggings away, tossing them aside before going for my lace thong, and the second he has me naked in his bed, all bets are off.

Spreading my thighs, he lowers his mouth to my mound, tracing his tongue through my delicate folds, swirling, licking, and sucking until my body shudders and I find myself forgetting how to breathe.

Reaching between my thighs, I run my fingers through his hair, tugging at his thick mane as I ride his tongue.

Hudson's arms hook around my legs, and his hand snakes up my belly, stopping at my swollen breasts.

"If you ..." I sigh. "If you keep doing this

… I'm going to … I'm getting close …"

He stops.

Just like that.

My pussy aches, throbbing for his touch, silently begging for him to put out the fire he so greedily started.

Moving to his nightstand, he pulls a gold foil packet from the top drawer, placing it between his teeth and ripping it open. Sheathing his cock, he comes back to me.

Positioning himself between my legs, he drags the tip of his cock against my slick seam. Back and forth, slow and tortuous. I suck in a breath, harboring it in anticipation, and without warning, he guides every inch of his thick cock inside me, pressing himself all the way in and leaving no part of me untouched.

Pushing himself over me, his lower body moves with an insatiable rhythm, taking from me everything he can and giving to me everything he's got. My fingers dig into his lower back, clenching at his muscled body with each insertion.

Hudson kisses me again, claiming my mouth for his own.

"God, you feel so good," he moans, grazing his lips on mine and breathing us in.

Without warning, Hudson pulls out, rising on his knees before guiding me to my stomach. With his hands on my hips, he pulls my ass toward him, propping me up before aligning himself.

Dragging his cock against my seam, he presses himself in with one hard thrust, and I clench a fistful of his thousand-thread count sheets.

He fucks me from behind, his thrusts animalistic and demanding, and I'm grateful. I'm grateful because for a moment there, the sex was sweet and tender and passionate.

And I just can't …

Not with him.

Not now.

Not under these circumstances.

Steadying myself, I fuck him back, thrust for thrust, all but giving my body to him on a shiny silver platter. That's all he wants anyway. It's not my heart he's after.

Besides, I don't want his either.

Clenching my eyes, I ride the wave the first

chance I get, letting myself succumb to the seismic orgasm pulsing through my core as he pistons harder, faster, finally finishing.

I collapse, and he leaves, heading to his bathroom to clean up. When he returns, I drag myself up, brushing my hair from my face and hoping I can make it to the door without my legs giving out beneath me.

"Where are you going?" he asks, crawling back in bed.

"Back to my room."

"Stay," he says.

Chapter Sixteen

Hudson

"Mr. Rutherford?" Savannah/Shoshannah taps on my door Friday morning, her fingers fidgety like she doesn't know where to put them when they're not in use.

I glance through the clear glass door, lifting a brow.

She knows not to bother me when my door is closed, but I'm trying to cut her some slack here because I don't feel like listening to another one of Mari's lectures.

Forcing a modest smile, I nod. "Yes, come in."

"Thank you," she says, exhaling and smiling.

"For what?"

"Thank you," she repeats, "for the flowers. They're beautiful. And I accept your apology."

I have no idea what the fuck she's talking about.

"And thank you for spelling my name correctly," she adds with a relieved titter. "On the card. It means a lot. I know you're not the best with names."

Mari.

All of this screams of Mari's doing.

"You're welcome, Sa … Shoshannah." I force a smile and politely wave her out. "Now, if you don't mind, I'm in the middle of something right now."

"Of course," she says, prancing away like a nervous Pekingese at a dog show.

Turning back to my computer, I flick my pen back and forth and lose myself in thought. I hate the second round of revisions. That township in Jersey felt the library needed a little something extra, though they couldn't say what. That's my job, they said. Never mind that I'm not a mind reader, and I don't particularly enjoy wasting my valuable time playing guessing games.

Besides, this building is absolutely perfect just the way it is.

But if they want something extra … I'll give them something extra. At the end of the day, they're not *my* taxpaying dollars going to waste.

We're leaving for Montauk this afternoon, and this project was supposed to be finished by now, but so much for that. Looks like I'll be taking work with me, and I'm sure my mother will find every excuse she can to ensure that I know how disappointed she is.

Today's weather is abnormally cheery, which is distracting for me, so I make my way around my office, yanking the blinds down until it's dark so I can focus. Flicking on my desk lamp, I try to concentrate on this fucking library one more time, but I'm feeling rather uninspired.

Believe it or not, I'm actually looking forward to spending a few weeks by the ocean with Mari.

Grabbing my phone, I dial her up so I can chew her ass while I'm thinking of it.

"Hey," she answers on the third ring. "What's up?"

"What are you doing?" I ask.

"Did you seriously just call me to see what I'm doing? What are you, my fiancé or something?"

The phone rustles. "I'm packing. We're still leaving today, right?"

"Right," I say. "Mari, what did you send to my assistant today?"

"Oh? She got the flowers?"

"Why'd you do that?" My jaw tenses.

"Because you owed her an apology. And because I want the two of you to be on good terms before you take off for an entire month," she says. "It's the right thing to do."

"In the future, I'd appreciate if you wouldn't meddle in my work affairs," I say. "And before you send *any* woman flowers in *my* name, at least have the decency to run it by me first."

"Whatever." She laughs.

"I mean it."

"Get back to work," she says. "I'm hanging up now."

The second she ends the call, my line rings.

"Yes?" I answer, exhaling. I could have sworn I pushed the "do not disturb" button hours ago.

"You have a visitor, Mr. Rutherford," Shoshannah says.

Glancing at my iCal, I don't spot any appointments.

"I thought I asked you to keep today clear? It's my last day in the office before my vacation. It's very important that I have zero interruptions," I say, pushing a breath past my nostrils before rubbing my left temple.

"She's not on the schedule, Mr. Rutherford."

She?

Oh, God. Tell me it's not Sienna.

I wouldn't put it past her to show up here after the string of text messages she sent a little bit ago. She's got a temper, that one. I used to pick fights with her on purpose because contrary to popular belief, two adults can still have hot makeup sex without being in an actual relationship.

"I'll be out in a second." I replace the receiver and straighten my tie, cleaning up my workspace before heading down the hall to the reception desk. I'm going to have to turn her away, and it's going to be painful for the 'old' me, but it is what it is.

By the time I round the corner, I see that God has in fact answered my plea.

It's not Sienna.

"Audrina," I say. "What are you doing here?"

"Hudson." She slinks past the front desk; lanky arms open wide as her hips sway. Before I can stop her, she's wrapping herself around me and kissing my cheeks. "It's so good to see you. Can I steal you away for just a moment?"

I lead her back to my office and close the door.

"What are you doing here?" I ask.

"Just in the city for some last minute shopping before I head to Montauk," she says, her green eyes flashing and mesmerized as she takes me in. "I wanted to stop by and personally congratulate you. I heard about your engagement."

"Good news travels fast."

"I'm looking forward to meeting the lucky woman." Audrina's voice falters. She smiles, but her shoulders droop and she glances off to the side for a brief second. "You're going to be thirty in a couple of weeks."

"I know."

"Remember what we always said? What you always *swore* to me?"

"Yes."

"If we were both unmarried by thirty, we'd marry each other." Her lips pull into a hesitant smile, and she tucks a strand of silky chocolate hair behind her ear.

"We were kids when we said that, Audrina."

"I'd hardly call us kids when we made that promise," she corrects me.

"I'm in love. I'm marrying Maribel. I'm sorry."

"Who is this girl anyway, Hudson?" Audrina winces. "I saw you last Christmas. You were single and loving it. How could someone pin you down and make you the marrying type in under five months? The timing's rather suspect, don't you think? Especially since we both turn thirty this summer ..."

She laughs, though I see the pain in her eyes. Despite it all, I have zero sympathy for her.

"You'll meet someone eventually," I say,

monotone, as I direct my attention toward my laptop and take a seat. "I'm sure."

Audrina huffs, rolling her eyes and blinking away tears. She looks admittedly lovely today, dressed to the nines in a floral, bare-shouldered sundress, nude espadrilles, and a tiny Fendi clutch, and I'm positive she put herself together for my sake.

"You know," she says, her tone wistful. "Your mom is throwing that engagement party this weekend. And I can't stop thinking about how it should've been us."

"You're clearly not hearing me."

"This was going to be *the* summer, Hudson." She shakes her head. "I thought we were going to finally get back on track. We belong together and you know it."

"Audrina."

"Do you know how many men I've turned away? How many proposals I've walked away from over the years because I was holding out for *you*?" Her complexion turns ruddy, her eyes misty again.

"Don't put that on me," I snort, shaking my head.

"You *promised*, Hudson." She shakes her head, rising. "Shame on me for thinking you were a man of your word. All you do is lie. All you do is tell people what they want to hear so you can get what you need from them. I hope this *Maribel* knows that about you."

Audrina heads to the door, stopping with her hand on the knob.

"I'm sorry," I say again. "It's just not meant to be. You need to accept that so you can finally move on."

She scoffs. "What am I supposed to do? If I could snap my fingers and fall out of love with you, don't you think I would? Loving you, Hudson, for all these years, has killed me. And now I have to show up at your parents' house and smile like I'm happy for you."

"You don't have to go." I shrug. "Feel free to sit this one out."

"Ha." She rolls her eyes. "You know as well as I do that my absence will only make things more awkward for everyone. Your family, my family, everyone knows it was always supposed to be you and me. If you're all of a sudden engaged and I fail to show up, it'll make *me* look bad. And I refuse to be a laughingstock all because you think you've met

The One."

"I'm glad you can be an adult about this." I rise, shoving my hands in my pockets and keeping my distance. Audrina has always been a bit of a loose cannon: sophisticated and charming one minute, venom-spewing and tantrum-throwing the next. "I know Maribel looks forward to meeting everyone."

Audrina's mouth pulls up at one side, though it isn't a happy smirk. It's more devious.

"And I look forward to meeting her," she says.

With that, she's gone.

Chapter Seventeen

Mari

"Do you think we're ready for this?" I climb into the back of Hudson's limo as Rocco loads our bags Friday afternoon. "I feel like we've been spending all this time together, but I still don't feel like a couple, It doesn't feel authentic. What if they see through us?"

Hudson takes my hand, kissing the top before pulling me closer.

"Relax," he says. "This isn't like you to be so … worked up."

"How would you know? You've only known me two months."

He chuckles. "I've come to know you well these last couple of weeks, Mari. You're intelligent. You have a great sense of humor. And you tend to go with the flow. All you have to do is be yourself these next few weeks—in addition to pretending to be madly in love with me— and the hard part will be over."

Rocco closes the trunk with a gentle push and slips into the driver's seat, merging into traffic a minute later.

Hudson's right.

This isn't like me to be so nervous. I just have a bad feeling that I can't explain. It's like this heaviness is sinking into me, weighing me down. My stomach was churning earlier, and I found myself unable to stop pacing the confines of my bedroom, my skin on fire and my breath shallow.

I called Isabelle, but she insisted it was probably pregnancy hormones and that I should call my doctor, which I was in the midst of doing until Marta barged in with a question about Hudson's packing list—like I would have the answers anyway.

But I don't think it's hormones.

It's nerves. Or maybe it's the universe's way of telling me it's not too late to back out as long as I do it now.

"Here." Hudson hands me a chilled bottle of Fiji water from a built-in cooler.

I remove the cap and try my hardest not to

chug the entire thing in one go. The forecast today was calling for a high in the upper seventies, but it may as well be a scorching ninety-nine degrees the way my body's behaving.

Fanning myself, I press the window button until the glass drops and I'm greeted with a burst of tepid city air.

"Mari." Hudson laughs. "Good God. You need to stop getting yourself worked up. My family doesn't bite. I promise."

Turning to him, I swallow a lungful of air and take a generous swig of water. "It's one thing to toss a ring on my finger and buy me a new wardrobe and meet my parents and take me on a few dates and kiss me and ... everything else ... but—"

"Mari, Mari. Stop." Hudson scoots closer, placing my water in a nearby cup holder and taking both of my hands in his. It's sweet, the way he's trying to calm me down, and I still find myself wondering if I'm imagining this kinder side of him or if it's been here all along. "Everything's going to be fine. We can do this. You and me. We've got this."

***

The limo crawls to a stop outside a wrought iron gate about three hours later. I can't see beyond the wall of manicured shrubs and towering foliage, but I imagine what lies on the other side is nothing short of majestic.

A sign on the left reads *Sea La Vie – A Private Residence*. Rocco presses a call button, and within seconds, the heavy, polished gates welcome us in.

"Sea La Vie." I read the sign quietly. "Cute."

"It was my great-grandmother's idea," Hudson says. "This home has been in the family for generations."

He gives my hand a squeeze before clearing his throat and narrowing his brows. It's taken me this long to realize he changed out of his suit and tie get up and into a pair of crisp navy chinos and a white button down covered in a gray cashmere sweater. He's finished the look with a pair of boat shoes, and he looks every bit the part of a Hamptons resident.

Glancing down at my ensemble, which

184

consists of a white eyelet shift dress, nude sandals, and a floppy beach hat, I realize I do too.

Rocco navigates the limo around a circular drive. A bubbling sculpture fountain temporarily distracts me until we pass into the shadow of the mammoth estate. Covered in weathered shingles and three times as wide as it is tall, I have to wonder if *Sea La Vie* comes complete with its own zip code.

"Four ... chimneys?" I ask. "Is one of them just for looks?"

I crack a chuckle, but clearly my Titanic joke falls on Hudson's deaf ears.

Rocco wastes no time climbing out and grabbing the door for us, and the moment I step onto the brick-paved drive, the front doors swing open and a smiling Helena ushers her way toward us with open arms.

"Hudson," she says, moving toward her son first. She deposits sweet, grazing kisses onto his cheeks before cupping them in her hands. "You look rested, dear."

Rocco unloads our luggage and Helena strides toward me. It's only when she takes my hands in hers and tilts her cherry face that I wonder if this is remotely the same woman I met before.

"It's very nice to see you again, Maribel. I'm so glad you could join us," she says. Hooking her arm into mine, she leads us past a woman dressed in a black and white maid's uniform and through the main doors, which are even bigger than they looked from the driveway.

"Thank you for having me," I say, trying not to gape at the sweeping entrance and the unobstructed view of the ocean. Two curved staircases flank the foyer, and straight ahead lies a wall of windows and sliding doors leading to a covered patio with billion dollar views. "Your home is lovely."

"Why, thank you. You're very kind to say that." Helena places her hand over her chest, and I wonder how many times she's had to pretend to be humble in this home. I don't even think the Dalai Lama could be humble in a place like this.

"Mrs. Rutherford, where would you like me to take the bags?" Rocco asks from the doorway.

"Oh, yes. Hudson will be staying in the Roosevelt room," she says it so nonchalant, like it's nothing, like everyone names their bedrooms after dead presidents. "And we'll be putting Maribel in the Kennedy suite."

"Separate rooms, Mother?" Hudson

chuckles, lifting a brow. "Is that really necessary?"

Helena's smile fades. "It's all in good taste. Anyway, I'm going to show Maribel to her room. Why don't you meet us on the patio in a little while? The Sheffields will be here soon. I know they're dying to meet our guest of honor."

Helena links her arm in mine once more and leads me up the left-hand staircase, past a long hallway with portrait-covered walls, around a corner, down another endless hallway, until we stop outside a polished wooden door flanked by ocean-view windows.

With a quick twist of the door knob, she flicks the door open, her lips smiling wide as her hands lift at her sides.

"Welcome to the Kennedy suite," she says, proud. The room, shaped like half of a hexagon, has sweeping views of the sea below, a gorgeous four-poster bed, a writing desk, and a sky-high ceiling. "You have a private bath. This way."

Helena takes me into a bathroom clearly ripped from the pages of *Veranda* magazine. I trace my fingertip along the white marble counters before eyeing the sparkling claw foot tub in the corner, resting beneath a crystal chandelier.

If I didn't know any better, I'd say Helena gave me the best room in the house. Maybe it's her way of apologizing for our last encounter?

"I hope you'll be comfortable during your stay," she says, turning to me.

I don't realize it until I try to respond, but my jaw is hanging wide open.

"This room, this suite," I say, eyes wide. "It's stunning. Thank you so much, Helena."

"Almost forgot," she says, placing a finger in the air and striding back to the bedroom. "These flowers are for you."

I hadn't noticed the giant bouquet of white peonies until she said something.

"You'll have fresh flowers in your room each week during your stay," Helena bends slightly, bringing her nose to the top of a stem. "If you prefer another type of flower, just let me know."

"Peonies are my favorite."

"A girl after my own heart." Helena winks. I think I like Helena now ... at least this version of her. I can only hope it's genuine.

"I wanted to tell you," she says, placing her

hand over her heart, "how truly sorry I am for the way I must have seemed when we first met. I guess … I guess I was in shock? And I felt somewhat disappointed that my only child had kept such a big, important announcement a secret from me. I didn't mean to be so cold to you, Maribel. I hope you can forgive me."

"He wasn't keeping it a secret," I say. "He was waiting for the right time to tell you. He wanted to announce it here, in front of everyone."

"Well, either way." Her eyes widen before squinting. "I wasn't my best self that day, and for that, I apologize. I look forward to getting to know you, dear. You must be something special for my son to finally take himself off the market."

"Thank you, Helena. I look forward to getting to know you as well."

We stand in silence, each of us eye to eye, and then she nods.

"Okay, well, I'll let you get settled. Please join us outside when you're ready," she says. "My husband should be back from town any moment with the lobsters. He can't wait to meet you."

Helena shows herself out, closing the door when she leaves, and I sink into the middle of a down-covered bed, surrounded by a million fluffy pillows.

This is heaven on earth.

Literally.

I don't ever want to leave.

A gentle knock at the door pulls me out of my Cinderella moment, and I spring up, adjusting my hat and brushing my hair back into place.

"Come in," I call.

The door cracks open and Hudson steps in. "Just checking on you. Is this room going to be okay?"

"Are you kidding me?" I rise, moving to him, and I can't stop smiling. "This is the nicest room I've ever seen in my entire life."

He laughs, like he thinks I'm joking.

I'm not.

"I could live here," I say. "Forever."

"Let's not get ahead of ourselves."

I roll my eyes. "You know what I mean."

"She put you in the east tower," he says.

"Is that a bad thing?" I arch a brow.

"You're going to be over here all alone." He slips his hands into his pockets and moves toward the windows. "Everyone else stays in the south wing. Or the guest house."

"Maybe she just wanted to give me privacy? I'm not going to complain about this room," I say with a sigh. "I mean, how could I? Look at that view."

"You should see the views from my room."

"Are you trying to give me a complex? Your mother was nice enough to put me up in this beautiful suite and apologize for the way she behaved the first time we met," I say. "Don't make me second-guess her intentions or it's going to be a long four weeks."

Hudson comes closer, taking my hands in his and pressing his body nearly against mine. "Just wish you were closer to me, that's all."

I tilt my head, chuffing. "You don't have to do this. No one's watching."

"I don't have to do what?"

"Pretend."

"I'm not pretending. I wish you were closer," he says, eyes searching mine.

"Why? For booty call purposes?"

"Booty call? Do people even use that term anymore?"

I roll my eyes again, and he slips his hands around my waist. Breathing him in, my heart skips a hard beat before settling into a quick rhythm.

"I have absolutely no idea what you're doing." I say, half-teasing, half just being honest. "Why do I feel like you want to kiss me right now?"

"I want to do a lot more than just kiss you right now." He snickers, his hand sliding up my arm before settling just beneath my jaw. Angling my mouth toward his, he brings his lips close but goes no further. "I know what you are to me, Mari. And I know what this is. But having you here is like this … breath of fresh air … that's the only way I know how to describe it. And your body in this dress … and my mother placing you just a hair out of reach … is pure fucking torture."

"Like you had a chance anyway."

"Like I had a chance? Mari, I've already had you," he says. "But I want you again."

"What makes you so sure the feeling's mutual?"

"If I kissed you right now," he asks, "would you make me stop?"

The warmth of his lips graze mine, though he hasn't kissed me. Not yet.

Someone clears their throat in the corner, and our lust-filled gazes dart in that direction.

"Hello, Mother," Hudson says.

"The Sheffields have arrived. Please make yourselves presentable and join us downstairs." Helena disappears before I have a chance to read her expression, and I was too embarrassed to make eye contact.

"Oh, god." I bury my face in my hands.

"Trust me, that was more awkward for her than it was for us," he says, pulling my hands down. "But we shouldn't keep them waiting."

He leads me down the hallways and corridors and around corners until we get to the curved staircase where laughter echoes off the white-washed walls and double-height foyer ceiling.

"There he is!" A round-bellied man in

country club attire waddles toward Hudson, arms open wide. "Hudson, it's been too long. Haven't seen you since ... this time last year."

The man laughs at his own joke and reminds me of a retired uncle who probably golfs for breakfast, lunch, and dinner.

"Good to see you, Duke." Hudson pulls me close.

"Is this ...?" A woman in sleek, sun-bleached hair and a vintage Emilio Pucci maxi dress sashays in our direction, her fingers lifting to her lips and an enormous diamond glinting in the natural sunlight.

"My fiancée," Hudson says, tossing me a wink. "Duke and Cybil Sheffield, meet Maribel Collins."

"Well isn't she a pretty little thing?" Cybil's excited tone is forced as she steps in and air kisses my cheek, and she keeps a careful distance. I can't help but feel like she's sizing me up, comparing me to her daughter. "Audrina, meet Hudson's *future wife*."

She says "future wife" like the words leave a curious taste in her mouth, but Hudson gives my hand a reassuring squeeze.

"So you're the *lucky* girl." Audrina's eyes glaze over me, head to toe as she squares her shoulders. She's pretty, in a mean-girl sort of way. Too pretty, almost. Life's been generous to her. Silky, chocolate hair drips down her shoulders, and her skin is flawless, lacking so much as a single worry line or premature wrinkle. Hooking a hand on her bony hip, her bee-stung lips arch into a devious smile. "Welcome to the family."

Chapter Eighteen

Mari

I feel like now wouldn't be the best time to tell Helena I'm not the biggest fan of seafood, so I bite my tongue and decide to suffer through.

It's just one dinner.

One of many.

I'm sure I'll be downing all kinds of New England fare over the next few weeks, and I might as well learn to appreciate some properly cooked, freshly caught seafood.

Helena prances around the kitchen in an unstained blue gingham apron with white lace trim, peering over the shoulders of one of the chefs as he drops a live lobster into a pot of boiling water.

I reach for a glass of water and look away.

I can't.

"Would anyone like another glass of wine?"

Helena returns to the table, a bottle of red in her left hand and a bottle of white in her right.

"Yes, please." Audrina holds her glass by the stem. "You always have the best wines, Helena. Your collection is second to none."

"You're too sweet," Helena says. "Conrad and I picked this one up the last time we were in Monaco."

"You know I've still never been," Cybil says, waving her hand.

"That's insane. You know you're missing out. It's the most beautiful place." Helena waves her hand back at Cybil. "And Princess Grace."

They both utter a collective sigh, and I pretend not to be bored out of my mind. But it isn't their fault. I've never been a huge fan of small talk.

"So, Maribel." Audrina turns to me, twisting her wine goblet between her manicured fingers. "What do you think of Sea La Vie so far?"

"It's beautiful." I take a sip of water, and she watches me closely.

"First time in the Hamptons?" she asks.

I nod.

"Not a fan of wine?" Audrina asks, only her voice grows an octave louder, causing Cybil and Helena to cut their conversation short and glance my way.

I pull my shoulders back and smile. "I don't drink."

"Oh." Audrina lifts her brows, her green eyes round. "I suppose it's not polite to ask, but there aren't a lot of people our age who don't enjoy the occasional glass of wine …"

No. It's not polite to ask.

What if I were a recovering alcoholic? What if I were on some special medication that didn't mix well with alcohol?

She knows what she's doing.

"I just … don't drink." I place my water glass aside and offer her a modest smile.

She doesn't buy it, but I don't care.

Two can play this game.

The men step inside from the patio, smelling of expensive cigars and sea salt air. Hudson's father, Conrad, glances my way, giving me a warm smile.

I like him.

I met him shortly after the Sheffields arrived, and I think he could tell I was put on the spot, so he took the heat off me and told them some story about some mutual friend of theirs. As the Sheffields were shown to their suites, he pulled me aside and told me that he looked forward to getting to know me and hopes I'll be comfortable during my stay.

And he meant it, too.

His blue eyes, the ones that match Hudson's fleck for fleck, crinkled at the corners and his tone was cordial and confident, like a man who means what he says and doesn't have time for petty games.

Hudson takes the seat between myself and Audrina, slipping his arm around the back of my chair. Leaning closer, his lips brush against my ear.

"You doing okay?" he whispers.

It's sweet that he cares.

"Totally fine," I whisper back.

When I lean away, I catch a glance of Audrina from my periphery, her stare lingering on the two of us before she flicks her attention toward her wine glass and takes a generous taste.

"The lobster will be done soon," Helena tells the men. "Please have a seat. I hope you brought your appetites."

Duke rubs his bulbous belly and plops down into the seat next to Conrad at the head of the table. Cybil and Helena yammer on about vintage tiaras, which I'm assuming was one of the subjects they studied at boarding school back in the day because they both seem to know an awful lot.

"How could you not like the Strathmore Rose?" Cybil's jaw drops.

"I just find it a little … anti-climactic for my taste." Helena swirls her red wine, shaking her head. "Now, give me the Pearl Poire and you've got my attention."

Cybil laughs. "Of course."

"Audrina, you seem bored." Helena rests her cheek on her hand. "Your brother will be here tomorrow. That'll keep you good and entertained."

The ladies laugh, but Audrina stares ahead, toward the sun setting on the sea, slightly wistful, slightly lost in thought.

"Can't wait," she says, monotone.

"Oh, come on. You haven't seen your

brother in months," Cybil says. "I know you two miss each other, even if you won't admit it."

"How's he doing, by the way?" Hudson asks. "Saw him in the city not too long ago, but then he said he had to go overseas for work."

Cybil sighs. "Yes, if only Alec could stay in one place for more than a weekend or two."

Helena chuckles. "Can't blame him for living his life, now can we? He's young and the entire world is at his fingertips." Her eyes dart to me. "Maybe one of these days, Alec will meet a lovely young woman like Maribel and decide that planting roots is more appealing than sowing wild oats."

"To God's ears, Helena." Cybil lifts her glass, toasting to Helena's suggestion, and the women push their chairs out one at a time before heading to the kitchen.

With Duke and Conrad deep in conversation at the far end of the table, it's just the three of us now.

"Hudson, I wanted to show you guys my newest masterpiece." Conrad rises from the head of the table. "Hurry, before your mother comes back and tries to stop me."

"Masterpiece?" I ask.

"My father makes those ships-in-a-bottle," he says, brushing his lips against my cheek. "I'll be back in a minute."

Hudson's absence is marked with a noticeable chill in the air, but I refuse to wallow in it.

"So, Audrina, where are you from?" I turn my attention to the Ice Princess.

Her dark lashes flutter, and she sits up straight. "Potomac, Maryland."

"Like the *Real Housewives*."

"The real what?"

"The *Real Housewives of Potomac*?" I ask. "It's a show? On Bravo?"

Her perfect, pointed nose wrinkles. "Never heard of it."

"Oh? Okay." I reach for my water glass, but it's empty. "So, how long have you known the Rutherfords?"

"My entire life." She swirls her goblet but doesn't take a drink. Resting her cheek on her hand, she stares ahead like she'd rather be anywhere but here.

"Where did you go to college?" I ask.

I wish she knew this was just as painful for me as it likely is for her, but at least one of us is trying.

"Seriously?" Audrina sniffs.

"What?"

"You really want to do this?" she asks.

I laugh, because this woman has to be joking.

"What are you talking about?" I ask.

"The whole getting-to-know you thing. It's lame. And I'm bored. Besides, anything you want to know about me, you can find out from Hudson. Sometimes I think he knows me better than I know myself."

Refusing to elaborate, she rises from the table and saunters away.

Before I have a chance to process what just happened, Hudson returns with the men and takes his seat next to me.

"Dinner's on its way," Helena announces

from the doorway before glancing to us. "Where's Audrina?"

I shrug. "She just … left."

"Typical Audrina," Hudson says under his breath before slipping his hand under the table cloth and resting it on my knee. Leaning in, he adds, "She has a penchant for the dramatic arts. Don't let her get to you."

Sitting up straight, I remind myself I'm here for one thing and one thing only.

I have a job to do.

And I'll be damned if I give a flying fuck what the Potomac Ice Princess thinks.

"Believe me, I won't," I whisper, feeling his steady gaze on me. All evening he's been looking at me like I walked straight out of the pages of this year's *Sports Illustrated* swimsuit edition.

"Cut it out, you two!" Cybil chuckles, seating herself across from us as the chefs bring plates of garnished, well-presented lobster. "God, you make me miss being young. Those were the days, weren't they, Duke?"

"What's that, dear?" Duke turns his focus from Conrad and slips his arm around his wife.

"These two," Cybil says, wearing a slow, wine-induced grin. "They remind me of us when we were young."

"Wait," Duke says, his brows meeting. "You mean … we're not young anymore?"

The entire table erupts into polite laughter at Duke's lame joke, and I realize just as a bright red crustacean is being placed before me that I have no idea how to eat this thing.

Shit.

Everyone is focused on their plates, their silverware tinkling against the china as the conversation evaporates into quiet chewing.

It looks so natural to them, like they've done this a million times before. I glance toward the head of the table where a bowl of dinner rolls rests, untouched, in front of Duke. If I had something else on my plate, at least I could look busy. Sitting here, staring at this cherry red cockroach-of-the-sea and clearly not eating it is going to be glaringly obvious the second these people take a break from cracking claws.

"I'll be right back," I say softly, leaning into Hudson.

"Everything okay?" he asks.

"Yeah. Fine. I'm going to go find Audrina and let her know we're eating." Excusing myself, I head for the nearest bathroom and retrieve my phone, quickly pulling up an online video on how to eat lobster.

When I leave, I bump into Audrina standing in the dimly lit hallway before a mirror, a small makeup compact in her hand as she presses powder into the skin around her nose.

"There you are," I say. "We're eating."

She shoots me a death glare, and it's only then that I see the red in her eyes.

"You've been crying." I take a step closer, though every part of me is screaming inside to let it go.

She doesn't want my sympathy.

She wants Hudson.

"How astute of you, Maribel." She snickers, rolling her eyes.

"I don't know what went down between you and Hudson in the past," I say, "but he's moved on and this wedding is happening, and it's really in everyone's best interest if we could all move forward with respect and kindness."

Audrina laughs. "God, you're pathetic. Do you hear yourself right now?"

My jaw clenches. I refuse to let this pompous bitch get the best of me.

"How well do you even know Hudson anyway?" Audrina turns to me, her emerald eyes halfway between a squint and a glare. "It's like you just came out of nowhere."

"I know him well enough to know I'm going to marry him." I raise my chin, folding my arms across my chest.

"He's not the marrying kind," she says, clicking her compact shut.

"Maybe he didn't use to be. People change all the time," I say. "From the moment I met him, he's shown me that people aren't always what they seem. And if you take the time to get to know them, sometimes you realize they're worth all the trouble they put you through."

"You've got that right." Audrina huffs, angling her body toward me and resting a hand on her hip. "Hudson's not what he seems. At all. We're all just ... pawns ... in his game. You'll see soon enough."

Footsteps send her gaze darting past my

shoulders, and I turn around to see Hudson entering the hall.

"Everything all right?" he asks, slinking up behind me and placing his hands on my hips.

Audrina's pouty lips twist into a sneer. "Always."

She excuses herself, her heels clicking across the hardwood until the sound grows distant.

"What was that about?" he asks.

Exhaling, I shake my head. "I think she's threatened by me. She doesn't want us together."

"Did she say that?"

"In not so many words," I say.

"That's not appropriate." His lips press flat. "I don't want her giving you any trouble, Mari. You'll tell me if she's bothering you, won't you?"

"She's not bothering me. I honestly don't care what she says or does or thinks or whatever." I unfold my arms. "And it's weird that you're being so protective of me."

"How is that weird? You're my fiancée."

"*Fiancée*," I remind him, placing air quotes

around the word as I speak it. I cock my head. "Anyway, I can hold my own. Trust me."

He releases a held breath, his blue eyes glinting with relief as his lips tug into a half-smirk. "That's … kind of sexy, Mari."

"Come on, let's go back." Rolling my eyes, I slip my arm into his. "And you're still not getting laid tonight."

Chapter Nineteen

Hudson

She's out cold.

And this teacup is seconds from burning the palm of my hand.

Placing the steaming mug on her nightstand, the bed shifts under my weight and Mari begins to stir. Pulling the covers to her neck, she releases a dreamy moan before rolling to her side.

It takes her a moment, but the second she realizes I'm next to her, she brushes the hair from her face and sits up with a startle.

"When did you come in here?" she asks, pushing up on her hands.

"Good morning." I reach for the tea, handing it over. "And a minute ago. You were sleeping. I didn't want to wake you."

One of the bay windows is cracked open halfway, and an ocean breeze ruffles the gauzy curtains. The sun is just beginning to rise over the water, painting Sea La Vie in a serene glow that feels like the summers of my youth.

"Thank you." She takes a sip of tea, cupping it in both hands when she's done and pulling her knees to her chest.

"Sleep well?"

"Like a dream." Mari nods, mouth tugging up at the sides. "What's the plan today?"

"Thought I'd take you to the market. We could pick up a few items for dinner later, maybe some local art. I don't know if you're into souvenirs or any of that," I say.

"Really?" She lifts a brow.

"Really, what?"

"Just surprises me that you're into that sort of stuff," she says. "You're so … metropolitan playboy. You're like an anti-tourist."

"I'm *not* into that sort of stuff," I say. "You're going to be here for the next four weeks, and I want you to get acclimated. Plus, believe it or not, this place can get kind of monotonous after a bit. Staying busy helps with that."

"You're the expert." She takes another sip before sitting the teacup on her nightstand and climbing out of bed. Stretching her arms overhead, the hem of her nightshirt rises, revealing the soft flesh of her lower belly. She doesn't have washboard abs by any means, but she's sexy just the same.

Sauntering to the dresser, she pauses before the mirror, finger-combing her hair into place.

"You just going to sit there and watch me get ready?" she asks, glancing up in the reflection to meet my gaze.

"Isn't that what couples do?" My mouth pulls into a teasing smirk, and I rise off her bed. "Anyway, I'll leave you now. Come downstairs when you're ready."

***

"That's right, I said *fifty* guests, not fifteen. Five-zero." My mother places her hand over the receiver of her phone, rolling her eyes. "On the phone with the venue for the engagement party. They can't seem to comprehend that we're going to need their largest party room plus full access to the private rooftop patio."

"I thought you said it was going to be a small gathering?" I ask.

She chuckles. "Fifty people *is* a small gathering, Hudson."

Moving to the hearth room just beyond the breakfast nook, I take a seat in an overstuffed chair with a sweeping view of the morning tide as it crashes on the rocky shore. One day this house will belong to me, though I haven't the slightest clue what I'd do with it. I won't have children to fill it with laughter. I won't have "couple" friends like my parents do, at least not ones I'd want to cohabitate with for a solid month straight.

I truly won't have any need for a place like Sea La Vie, and letting it sit empty for months upon months would be a travesty.

There's a melancholy sadness yet at the same time a quiet emancipation that floods my senses when I let that reality sink in.

"Good morning, darling." I hear my mother's voice from the table, and I glance over expecting to see Mari, only it's Audrina. "Did you sleep well?"

"Always, Helena." Audrina kisses my

mother's cheek before turning my way. "Good morning, Hudson." She slinks toward the hearth room, taking a seat across from me.

Dressed in a short yellow sundress that contrasts against her tan skin, she crosses her legs, letting the hem of her skirt slide up her outer thigh, but I refuse to play her little game. Instead, I focus on the rising tide past the picture windows.

"What are you and your lovely bride-to-be planning for the day?" Audrina asks, lashes batting.

"I'm taking Maribel to the market," I say, still avoiding eye contact.

"Ha." Audrina rolls her eyes.

"What?"

"That was always our thing," she says, pushing a quick breath through her nose. "The Saturday morning bazaar."

"Hey." Mari places her hand on my shoulder. "Ready to go?"

"Absolutely." I rise, taking her hand in mine but keeping my eyes locked on Audrina's suspicious glare.

***

"I want to know more about your childhood." Mari thumbs through a postcard rack beneath a vintage letterpress company's white tent. Turning to me, she adds, "I just feel like I'm seeing this side of you I never knew existed, and it makes me wonder what else is there."

"And my childhood has to do with it … why?"

"That's where it all begins. That's where you learn how to love and how to be loved. How to treat people, that sort of thing."

"You know I absolutely hate it when you try to psychoanalyze me." I pluck a postcard from a nearby rack and read the inscription on the back. It's used. Why anyone would want to buy an old, used postcard is beyond me.

"I'm not trying to psychoanalyze you," she says, holding up a card covered in lighthouses and bringing it closer for inspection. "I want to know what makes you tick. I'm beginning to think I had you all wrong from the start."

"In what ways?"

Mari places the postcard back and secures her bag over her shoulder. I follow her to the next tent, where she proceeds to buy a homemade cinnamon roll from a woman in a white apron.

"We're splitting this, by the way," she says, handing me a second fork as we walk away.

"In what ways did you think you had me wrong from the start?" I ask again.

"I don't think you're an asshole ... on purpose," she clarifies. "But I don't think that's who you are. I don't think it's inherent. I don't think you get off on being a jerk, I think it's just this suit of armor you wear because you've been hurt."

Clenching my hand over my heart, I chuckle. "Yes. Poor, broken me."

"I'm being serious," she says, shoving the cinnamon roll my way. "Hey, you're not eating enough of this."

I take a forkful just to appease her and we continue strolling past stand after stand, weaving through heavy morning crowds.

"I've seen this softer side of you, Hudson," she says, chewing. "I want to know where it came from. And why you try to hide it so much."

I chuff. "I wouldn't call myself *soft*."

"Of course *you* wouldn't," she says. "But you are. You have this kind side. You care for others, I've seen it. You don't make it into a big thing, but you're a good person—when you want to be. You're a good son. And you're a good fake fiancé."

"I know."

She laughs.

"Was it hard?" she asks, smile fading. "Being shipped off to school all the time?"

I roll my eyes. "Really? We're going to take about this here? Now?"

"I just keep thinking about it and what that would do to a child." She shakes her eyes, eyes almost misting.

"It's quite common in our circles," I say, posture rigid. "It's not something I ever cried about, at least maybe not past kindergarten."

"They shipped you off in kindergarten?" Her jaw falls. "But you were just a baby."

"Don't look at me like that, Mari."

"Like what?"

"Like you feel sorry for me."

"But I do. It's really sad," she says, sighing. "They kept you at an arm's length. They loved you from a distance. It explains everything." She takes another bite of cinnamon roll, chewing quickly before swallowing it all in one lump. "That laid the entire foundation for your adult love life. You realize that, don't you?"

I laugh. "What the hell are you talking about?"

"You're thirty years old and you've only ever had one girlfriend, right?"

"Right."

"And you prefer one-night stands, no-strings, casual hook ups, that sort of thing," she states it like it's a fact. "You don't do romance. You don't do relationships. You don't want to settle down or get married—at least not in the legitimate sense."

"What are you getting at?"

She stops cold, pointing her fork at me with a smirk on her face. "You don't feel worthy of real, true, unconditional love, therefore you push it away before you even have a chance to experience it. Boom. I'm a genius."

"Mari." My head tilts. She keeps walking.

"Why didn't I go into psychology or something? I totally figured you out in, like, under ten minutes."

"You're giving yourself way too much credit," I say.

"Here, finish this. I'm stuffed." She shoves the roll at me before heading toward a pop up boutique filled with handmade items for women and children. Trying on a hat, she finds a nearby mirror to check her reflection before yanking it off and moving to a display of turquoise jewelry.

Standing back, I observe as she moves from the jewelry to a stack of bangle bracelets before passing a display of muslin baby blankets covered in cutesy animal prints. She stops, as if they catch her eye, and I wonder, for a second, if Maribel wants a family of her own someday.

Maybe it's wrong of me to hold back her dreams in pursuit of my own. I can only hope setting her up with a lifetime of financial security will make it all worth it. After all, it's the only thing I really have to offer.

Chapter Twenty

Mari

"May I come in?" Helena knocks on my door late Sunday afternoon.

"Yes, of course," I call back, striding across my suite to meet her.

"I have something for you," she says, entering and closing the door behind her. Unclasping her hand, she reveals a pair of ivory pearl earrings on gold posts, each surrounded by a row of glistening diamonds. "These earrings used to belong to my grandmother."

Lifting my hand to my mouth, I say, "They're stunning."

"They're for you," she says, handing them over.

"Helena."

"My gift to you. An engagement gift, if you will."

"You don't have to do this," I say.

"I've been holding them aside all these years." Her red lips spread into a wistful smile. "Patiently waiting until Hudson found the right one. I always knew he'd get married one day. The boy doesn't like to be alone, even if he won't admit it. Deep down, there's a hopeless romantic in there, but I digress. Go on. Try them on."

Taking the earrings, I move toward the dresser, securing them on my ears and tucking my hair behind my ears.

"They're absolutely beautiful." I turn to show her. "Thank you, Helena."

"Will you wear them tonight? To the party?"

"Of course. Absolutely I will." I walk toward the closet, pulling out the little black dress I plan to wear tonight. "A match made in heaven."

A knock at the door interrupts our moment, followed by a woman's voice beckoning for Helena.

"Excuse me, dear," Helena gathers her dress in her hands and heads across the suite toward the door. Her voice is low as she speaks with one of her employees, and after a moment, she turns to me after checking her watch. "Alec Sheffield has arrived. If you'll excuse me, I need to see to it that he gets settled. I'll see you at Bleu Marina's for the party."

***

"You look amazing." Hudson places his hand on the small of my back as we head toward the black awning outside Bleu Marina's. The building is sailcloth white with bright blue awnings, two stories tall and backing to the ocean. A covered porch surrounds much of the outside, and gentle music wafts from a rooftop patio above.

It takes my eyes a moment to adjust to the dim lighting once we step inside, but Hudson leads the way, taking us straight back to one of the private rooms where a table is already filling with exquisitely wrapped gifts. Helena stands in the corner with a glass of champagne, chatting it up with a small group of women.

"There they are," she proclaims, lifting her glass.

All eyes are on us—me, really.

I smile, keeping my head high as a woman with sleek white hair and a downturned nose comes

222

at me.

"You must be Maribel," she says, looking me up and down. "I'm Dianna, Helena's cousin. Welcome to the family."

Her words are kind, but her face is frozen. I'm blaming Botox.

"Nice to meet you, Dianna," I say.

"Uncle Frederick couldn't make it?" Hudson asks.

Dianna rolls her eyes. "He's outside on the patio. Your father brought those Cuban cigars he likes."

"Of course."

"If you ask me, it's a bit tacky to light them before dinner, but what do I know?" Dianna laughs, but her eyes don't wrinkle. "Anyway, I better make my rounds. Congratulations, you two. You make a beautiful item."

"Champagne?" A young woman holding a tray of sparkling flutes approaches us, and Hudson instantly takes two.

Handing one to me, I briefly panic before realizing I don't have to drink it. I can simply hold it for a bit ... and maybe misplace it as the night progresses.

"I think most of us are here," Helena announces, her voice growing loud over the steady rumble of delicate conversation filling the room. "I've sent for the men. If you'll all have a seat, I'd like to begin the night with a toast to our future bride and groom."

A quick glance around the room shows guests arriving by the second, filling in. Laughing. Smiling. Chit-chatting. Some of them stare in our direction with curious gazes, others seem more concerned with making a grand entrance or showing off their latest jewels and red-bottomed shoes.

"Shall we find a seat?" Hudson takes me by the hand, leading me to the head of one of the longer tables where I immediately place my champagne glass in front of my empty place setting.

It feels good to sit.

I've been on my feet all day, and while I'm not exactly hauling around an eight-pound unborn child, it took more out of me than I ever could have anticipated.

The men begin to shuffle in, taking spots next to their wives and girlfriends, and Helena stands at the opposite end of our table, smiling proudly and waving them in.

"All right," she says. "Now that we're all here, I'd like to start out by first thanking you all for making it on such short notice. Hudson and Maribel's engagement came as a bit of a surprise to us—a pleasant surprise—and when I found out Bleu Marina's had a cancellation for tonight, the timing was absolutely divine." Lifting her flute, she continues, "Anyway, it means the world to me to see my son truly happy and in love, and while we're still getting to know Maribel, I can already tell she's going to be an excellent addition to the Rutherford family."

"Sorry I'm late," a voice whispers. I glance to my left, where Audrina places her hand on the empty chair beside me. The faint smell of expensive perfume floats from her tight, tan body, and her hair and make up were clearly done by professionals tonight. A tight red dress hugs her body enough so that her cleavage is lifted in the most tasteful way possible.

If I didn't know any better, I'd think she was trying to show me up at my own engagement party …

I glance at Hudson, but his attention is

honed in on Helena, who's still rambling on several feet away.

"…so if you'll all raise a glass to the lovely couple," Helena says. "I'd like to make a toast. To Maribel and Hudson, may you live happily ever after, always."

A few of the women release "oohs and ahs" and the delicate tinkle of stemware against stemware fills the space.

Glancing down, I spot a glass of water, but as I reach for it, I feel a quick kick under the table … on my left.

Squinting, Audrina says, "It's bad luck to toast with water, Maribel. Don't you know that?"

"Lucky for you, I don't believe in superstitions." I toss back a mouthful of water, finishing with a boastful smile that clearly annoys the living shit out of the Ice Princess.

But my moment of pride is short-lived, swallowed into a sinking black hole the second I see Hollis walk in the door.

"Alec!" Audrina waves to get his attention, motioning for *him* to take the seat beside her—and next to us.

Chapter Twenty-One

Hudson

"Always thought you'd end up with my sister." Alec leans against the bar at Bleu Marina's, his hand gripped around a cold stein of beer.

"Mari's great, isn't she?" Scanning the room, I spot her in the corner, chatting away with my great aunts Tipper and Winnie. I knew Mari would be able to handle herself with dignity and grace under all this scrutiny, but she's really gone above and beyond tonight.

In fact, shortly after the toast, she decided to make some rounds solo, getting up and personally introducing herself to the rest of the room. I lost her somewhere between my mom's college sorority sister and our former neighbor from Manhattan.

"There's something familiar about her," Alec says, squinting in her direction. "She reminds me of someone."

"Who?"

"No clue." He shrugs, taking another drink.

"God, please tell me you didn't drunk-swipe her on Tinder last time you were in town."

Alec laughs. "Probably not. But you never know."

Shaking my head, I place my empty beer glass on the bar. "I should go to her."

"Yeah," he says, chuckling. "Do the right thing, man. Don't make her fend off these upper crust assholes by herself."

Making my way across the room, I find Mari in the corner with my father's former business partner's ex-wife, who is still entangled in the same Hampton's social circle after all these years.

This place is like a fucking cult for social climbers.

"Hey." I lean in, surprising her with a kiss in front of Bitsy Hinkler, who clasps at her pearls. "Didn't mean to leave you hanging. I needed to catch up with Alec. Hadn't seen him in a while."

"It's fine." She places her hand on my chest.

We've been here a while now, at least a good hour, and I know my mother only has the party room booked until seven.

"You want to go upstairs to the roof? Get some fresh air?" I offer.

"Yeah," she says, biting her lower lip. "That sounds … great."

We excuse ourselves from Bitsy and head for the stairs, climbing to the rooftop where a small jazz ensemble is setting up. The smell of fried seafood and expensive cocktails mixes with salty ocean air, and we find a small high top table near an isolated stretch of railing.

"You're doing great," I say.

She brushes a strand of blonde hair from her eyes, turning to me. "You don't have to encourage me, Hudson. I'm not a dog."

"I know." I smirk. "You're a smart-mouthed woman. I just wanted to tell you that I see what you're doing. I notice it. And I appreciate it."

"Which is more than you could ever say when I was your personal assistant." She winks, but I know she's not entirely kidding.

I smirk. "I deserve that."

"Would we care for anything to drink?" A

Bleu Marina server approaches our table.

"No, thanks," Mari says, and at the same time I say, "Yes, please."

We exchange looks and she laughs.

"I guess we're good," I say. "Thank you."

"You could've ordered something."

I shrug.

"I have to say, this night isn't as painful as I thought it would be," I muse, my gaze settling on her again.

"You thought it was going to be painful?"

"Painfully boring." I glance at the ocean below and the long stretch of dock leading to rows of boats bobbing in the water. "That said, do you want to get out of here?"

She glances from side to side before resting her eyes on mine. "The party's not over yet. We can't just leave."

"Ninety percent of the guests are downstairs and drunk out of their minds since my mother felt our engagement party required an open bar," I say. "The other ten percent haven't so much as said hello to either of us. I doubt they'd care if we just

… disappeared."

"Fine." She rises, clasping her clutch and placing it just beneath her elbow. Her mouth twists into a relieved smirk. "But only because it's your idea, and a good fiancée wouldn't force her future husband to stick around if he's ready to go."

"I like the way you think." I leave the table, resisting the urge to playfully slap her on the ass, and we head downstairs to slip away. If my mother asks tomorrow, we made our rounds and said our goodbyes. It's not like anyone will remember much of tonight anyway with all the champagne being passed around.

Minutes later, we're climbing into the front seat of my father's vintage Alfa Romeo Giulietta and cruising down Montauk highway, the salty wind in our hair and the stark realization that I'm quite enjoying my time with Maribel.

A lot more than I thought I would—actually a lot more than I should.

Chapter Twenty-Two

Maribel

I dig my toes into the sand, staring out at a pitch-black ocean painted in golden Montauk moonlight.

"You cold?" Hudson grabs a spare serape blanket and wraps it around my shoulders, scooting closer. His hand rubs small circles into my back.

"Thank you." I pull the fabric tight around me, gathering a handful to hold it together.

An hour ago we came back from the party, changed into pajamas, and decided to sit on the beach for a bit.

I'm still reeling—for better or for worse— about the fact that my baby's father walked into the party tonight. I couldn't let myself react though. I had to hold my head high, slap a smile on my face, and do my job.

"So are you and ... Alec ... close?" I ask, the wind having its way with my hair.

"We were best friends growing up," he says, bending his knees and wrapping his arms around them as he stares at the sea. "Alec is a bit of a free spirit. I sort of stuck around the city after college. He never stayed in one place for very long."

"He seems nice," I say.

"He's a nice guy, yeah. Hard to believe he and Audrina are related, huh?"

I chuckle, silently relieved and simultaneously disgusted that my unborn child will have Audrina as an aunt.

That is … if Alec decides he wants to be in the baby's life.

A free spirit like him might not want an obligation like this.

My body shivers, and whether it's from the cold or the reality that there's a high chance I'm going to be flying completely solo on this mission, I'll never know.

"You want to head inside?" he asks, reaching for my ice-cold fingertips and warming them in his hand. "You're freezing."

I nod, waiting as Hudson rises before pulling me up beside him. He turns me to face him, our eyes locking as he cups my chin softly in his hand.

"What are you doing?" I offer a nervous, breathy laugh.

"Kissing you," he says it like it's a done deal, a non-negotiable declaration of his intentions.

"Why?"

His lips draw closer to mine, and I inhale the clean scent of his cologne as it emanates from his warm skin.

"Because I want to." His lips skim against mine. "Because I feel like it." He exhales. "And because I couldn't take my eyes off you all night, and I knew, Mari, that this moment was completely unavoidable."

"You're making this extremely complicated, Hudson."

He answers me with a kiss, his lips pressing against mine with an impatient greed, his fingers slipping behind my neck and knotting in my hair as he guides my mouth.

The lights above the porch on the back of Sea La Vie flick on, illuminating the large expanse of private beach which, a second ago, felt cozy and secluded … a little island of our own.

I pull away from him.

"They're home now." I gather the beach blankets in a hurry. "We should head in."

***

Rinsing my face in the marble sink of my suite bathroom, I blot it dry with a fluffy gray towel before lifting my fingertips to my mouth, tracing the places Hudson's lips resided moments earlier.

I don't know why he's doing this, but if he keeps it up, it's not going to end well for any of us. And despite the fact that I'm well aware, I can't deny how good it feels to be wanted by a man like him.

Just weeks ago, I used to ruminate about all the reasons I couldn't stand this man, and now I find myself quietly admiring his confidence and intelligence while I mentally replay that intense night we shared together in his bed.

Exhaling, I shake my head in the mirror.

This is wrong.

I can't let this go any further—at least not

physically.

A soft knock on my bedroom door sends my heart into a freefall and my thoughts scattering like leaves to the wind.

Fuck wrong.

Running across the room, I grab the door handle and pull it wide, unable to wipe the devilish grin off my face.

"Audrina." My smile vanishes.

"You're pregnant." She pushes past me, causing the door to swing open and slap against the wall.

Scrambling to close it, making sure no one's in the hall before turning back to her. Hands on my hips, I watch her pacing my room like a crazy person.

"It makes perfect sense," she says, though I'm not sure if she's speaking to me or just thinking out loud. "And it's the only reason Hudson would marry someone like you so quickly."

"Someone like me?" My jaw hangs. I hate this bitch.

"Plus you're not drinking. You toasted with

fucking water at your engagement party and you haven't so much as touched a drop of wine all weekend."

"I don't drink." I shrug, stating it with conviction.

"Sweetheart, I saw the tattoo on your ankle." Her tone is smug, and I want to rip that smart-assed smirk off her pretty little face. "You're not some conservative Mary Poppins."

"Tattoos have nothing to do with alcohol," I say. "And I'm not pregnant, so you can just put your little theory to rest."

She stops pacing in front of me, her eyes lowering to my belly.

For a fraction of a second, I consider flipping up the bottom of my shirt and showing off my still-flat belly, but I won't lower myself to her level. I don't have to prove anything to her, and my pregnancy is absolutely none of her business.

"You're lying," she says, eyes all crazy and tightening in on me as her lips pucker.

"Audrina, it's late," I say. "And I'm tired. And I don't have time for this, so just go."

I move to the door, pulling it open and

waiting, yawning.

"Still don't believe you," she says as she struts toward me. Stopping, her eyes fall to my stomach once more and she huffs. "You're so fucking full of shit, and it drives me fucking crazy that I'm the only one who can see right through you."

Laughing, I roll my eyes. "Goodnight, Audrina."

"They're going to find out," she blurts. Or is it a promise?

"Good*night*, Audrina."

Shutting and locking the door behind her, I press my back against the smooth wood and exhale the deep breath I'd held far too long.

Shit.

Chapter Twenty-Three

Mari

"We had sex, didn't we?"

A man's voice forces my heart to my stomach as I raid the Rutherfords' fridge at two in the morning. I've spent the better part of the last few hours tossing and turning, my mind refusing to turn off, and if that wasn't enough, my stomach said now was the perfect time for a late night snack.

Slamming the fridge door, I see Alec standing on the other side in nothing but slow-slung sweats. His hands rest on his hips and he wears a proud smirk.

"I thought you looked familiar," he says.

"I don't think we should tell Hudson. Not yet."

"Psh." He moves past me, yanking the fridge door open and hunching over as he scans the selections. "Secret's safe with me. I don't want things to get weird, you know?"

"Good. Yeah. Me too," I say, biting the inside of my cheek. "I mean, he should know eventually. But not yet."

"Does he really even need to know at all?" Alec grabs a carton of orange juice, unscrews the cap, and takes a chug before replacing it. As well-bred and old-moneyed as Alec is, he reminds me of a free-spirited frat boy now that I've spent more than an hour around him. "Honestly, Mari, and this is not meant to offend you in any way, but I hardly remember that night. I was drunk out of of my mind."

"Really? You didn't seem drunk."

"I can hold my liquor," he says. "Anyway, it was just a fling. Didn't mean anything. And now you're marrying one of my best friends. We're good, right?"

My jaw falls, and I want to tell him.

I want to tell him so badly.

My stomach knots with each passing second.

The time isn't right. Not yet.

"Of course we're good," I say, forcing a smile.

"You should do something about that." He points to my stomach.

"What?!" My hands cover my non-existent bump.

"Your stomach's growling."

"Oh." I laugh, exhaling. "Right."

Grabbing the milk, I move toward the pantry in search of cold cereal.

"You want some?" I offer a minute later, holding up a box of Frosted Flakes.

"Frosted Flakes are my jam. It's like you read my fucking mind, Mari." He grabs the spoons and bowls and I do the pouring. I can't help but wonder if he'll want to be involved in the baby's life and what kind of team we'd make, but I know better than to have any expectations at all regarding this ironic, messed-up little situation.

Taking a seat at the breakfast nook, we chow down as we stare off at the midnight waves breaking on the shore.

"It's so pretty out here, isn't it?" I ask. "I've never seen anything like it."

"You need to get out more."

I huff, head tilted. "Wasn't exactly born with a silver spoon. Didn't get a black American Express card on my eighteenth birthday."

"Contrary to how it must seem, I foot my own travel bills, *thankyouverymuch*." His spoon clinks against the bowl. "Or I should say my company does."

"What do you even do for a living?"

"Marketing and social media consultant," he says. "Basically all these old companies run by eighty year olds hire me to make their business relevant again. Which I do. And they pay me handsomely for it."

"Nice."

"What do you do?"

My grip tightens around my spoon. "I can't say."

"What do you mean you can't say?" He chuckles.

"I work for someone, helping them with something, but I'm not allowed to discuss it."

"Oh." He nods, scooping some flakes onto his silver. "You signed a non-disclosure."

"Exactly."

"As long as it's nothing illegal ..." he shakes his head. "There are a lot of unscrupulous people out there, Mari, just waiting to take advantage of nice, young women who only want to help. Or there are assholes who just like to throw money at their problems."

I examine Hudson in that context, and I realize that Alec has a point, only Hudson's asshole ways have seemed to dissipate lately, so there's that.

"Anyway." Alec rises, taking his dishes to the sink before yawning. "Thanks for the cereal. Don't know about you, but your little party wore me out."

Wish I could say the same.

"Goodnight, Alec," I say. He waves, turning to leave. "Wait."

"Yeah?" He glances over his shoulder.

"Why'd you tell me your name was Hollis when we first met?"

"It's my middle name," he says, lips bunching together as he shrugs. "I didn't think it was that big of a deal. Tons of people use other names when they hook up."

"Yeah, but what if something happened and someone needed to find you again?"

"Why would anyone need to find me after a hook up? And why would I *want* anyone to find me after a hook up?" He chuckles, eyes focusing on me in the dark. "That's the beauty of a one-night stand."

"Forget it." I rise, gathering my dishes. "Goodnight, Alec."

Chapter Twenty-Four

Hudson

"I know you knocked her up." Audrina pokes her finger into my chest, her strong perfume assaulting my senses Monday morning as I close the fridge door and slam my carton of orange juice on the counter.

"It's way too early for this shit." I walk away from her, chuckling to myself. "And I didn't knock her up."

"She's *so* pregnant." Her voice fills the expansive kitchen, echoing off the walls. "It's ridiculously obvious to anyone with half a brain cell."

"*Shhh...*" I silence her. "Keep your voice down."

"Why? You don't want everyone to know?" Her tongue pokes her inner cheek as she wears a childlike grin.

"No, because I don't want you starting unnecessary rumors." I retrieve a juice glass from a cupboard and fill it to the top. "Mari's not pregnant. Think I would know."

"Why doesn't she drink?"

I huff. "Every woman who doesn't drink is automatically pregnant?"

Audrina's brows narrow as she searches for a rebuttal. "Why are you in such a hurry to marry her?"

"Because I fucking love her." I take a leisurely sip.

"But why the rush?"

"Because I fucking love her," I repeat.

"But you've always been so anti-marriage," she says. "Your social life is like a real life version of *The Bachelor*, only there's no ring and no proposal at the end and you screw everyone."

"I'm not allowed to change?" I lift a brow. She's quiet. "Your points aren't valid, Audrina. Please. Stop before you embarrass yourself any further."

"I'm not embarrassed," she says, crossing her arms across her fake tits. "I just don't understand why everyone's so head over heels in love with this girl who's clearly hiding something."

I chuckle, downing the rest of my juice before rinsing it in the sink. "And what makes you think she's hiding something, Detective?"

Audrina throws her hands in the air, fists clenched as she moans. "God, it's like I'm the only person in this entire fucking house with their feet rooted in some semblance of reality."

"Not true." I step closer to her, peering down my nose. "You're just bitter, Audrina. You're bitter that it's not you I'm marrying, and you're comparing yourself to her because you're insecure. You've always been insecure. It's one of the many, many reasons we've always been all wrong for each other."

Her jaw hangs, lashes fluttering as she tries to form a response, only Mari shuffles in from around the corner.

"Morning, gorgeous." I slip my arm around her, kissing her forehead.

"Ugh." Audrina waves her hand at us before spinning on her heel and all but stomping off.

"What's that about?" Mari asks.

"You're not going to fucking believe this," I

say, dragging my hand along my smirking mouth. "She thinks you're pregnant."

Mari's expression fades, turning to ash. I can only imagine how embarrassing it would be for her if my family believed the only reason I was marrying her was because she was pregnant and not because we're "madly in love." Not that it's the 1950s and those types of things are frowned upon, but because no one likes to be accused of something that isn't true.

It boils down to respect.

And ensuring Mari is comfortable during her stay here—not the brunt of Audrina's jealous rage.

"I set her straight," I say, slipping my hands around her waist and pulling her body against mine. "She's trying to figure out why we're in such a rush to get married, and apparently that's the only thing that makes sense to her."

"She's still in love with you." Mari's eyes search mine, though I'm not sure what she's looking for.

Shrugging, I roll my eyes. "And?"

"And she's not going to give you up that easily. That's the impression I get anyway," Mari says. "She wants to make this difficult for us."

"Let her. There's *nothing* she can say or do to derail this."

Chapter Twenty-Five

Mari

"First time sailing, Mari?" Conrad inspects the lines of his boat, apparently named *Seas the Day*, as Duke wrangles the flapping sails Monday morning.

"It is." I shield my eyes from the sun as Hudson steps on then turns to offer me his hand.

Audrina's seated a few feet away, next to Alec, paging aimlessly through this month's issue of *Harper's Bazaar*. She's wearing oversized, pitch-black sunglasses but I'm almost positive she's rolling her eyes.

"Where are your boat shoes?" she asks, glancing up from a glossy editorial. "You can't walk around in those sandals. You're going to slip."

"She'll be fine," Alec says. "Hud'll take care of her."

Hudson takes me by the elbow, and I glance around, noting the lack of seating aside from the captain's seats toward the middle. Leading me around the massive jib, we take a seat across from Audrina and Alec and wait for Helena and Cybil to make their grand entrance.

"We're going to be here all day if I don't lend a hand. Excuse me, Mari. I'll be back." Hudson joins his father and Duke, leaving me alone with my baby's father and his sister.

"You nervous at all?" Alec asks, squinting into the sun.

"No," I say. "Should I be?"

"Yes," Audrina huffs, biting a hidden smirk.

Alec nudges her. "No. Some people just get nervous on these. You're out on the open water, nothing but a life jacket and some flimsy railings keeping you safe. If you're not used to it, it might be scary."

"I have a feeling Conrad's done this hundreds of times," I say, turning to watch him tying some fancy knot on the other end of the vessel.

"He has." Alec nods. "He's an old pro. He and my father used to race these things in their younger days. That's how they met."

252

The wind picks up, sending the sailcloth flapping and drowning out our conversation, so Alec moves closer, taking Hudson's seat.

"Are you into sailing?" I ask.

His lips purse and he hesitates before shaking his head. "I get so fucking seasick on these things it's unreal, but it's just once a year, so I deal."

"Well that's gracious of you."

He smirks, revealing a set of dimples, and I can't help but to picture our child with the same ones.

"I try." He shrugs before pulling the Ray-Bans from his shirt collar and slipping them on.

Glancing toward Hudson, I catch him watching us, his eyes flicking back and forth between what he's doing and what we're doing.

"How long do you think we'll be out on the water?" I ask.

"All fucking day," Audrina chimes in, licking her index finger before flipping a page in her magazine.

"Most of the day," Alec says. "It's not that

bad, just work on your tan or something. It'll be over before you know it."

"I'm not trying to rush the experience, I was just curious," I say. "I'm actually excited. This is all brand new to me."

"The newness will wear off by noon," he says. "Trust me."

"Maybe." I shrug. "Maybe not."

"We're here, we're here," Helena announces, waving as her Lilly Pulitzer swimsuit cover up flounces in the wind. Cybil is a step behind her, carrying a large canvas tote packed full of food and drinks.

Hudson peers over at us again, unsmiling, and as soon as he's finished checking his line, he returns to my side, slipping his hand in mine. If I didn't know any better, I'd think he's jealous that I'm talking to Alec.

Sliding his phone from his pocket, Alec begins tapping the screen.

"No phones," Audrina says. "We're on vacation."

Alec huffs, ignoring her.

"What's more important than spending time with your sister and your best friend and his *lovely* fiancée?" She overemphasizes lovely, and I shoot her a look as my blood begins to heat. She's lucky we're in front of all these people and I'm too polite to make a scene.

"I'm checking on my flight," Alec says, chin tucked as he scrolls the screen.

"Where are you headed?" I ask.

"Hong Kong," he says. "I leave in two days."

"You're not staying the whole month like everyone else?" My heart races, and I'm speaking too fast. This isn't good. I thought I'd have more time with him … more time before I had to tell him.

"No, no." He chuckles. "I don't do that. I work for a living, unlike … five-eighths of the people on this boat."

"Oh." My throat constricts, and I make a mental list of all the things I need to do and say before he leaves. On top of that, I have no idea when—or if—I'm going to be alone with him at any point in the coming days. "How long will you be in Hong Kong?"

He dims his screen before slipping the

phone back in his pocket.

"Five, maybe six months?" he asks. "It all depends. Could be shorter, could be longer. I'm planning for six though."

I'm due in seven.

"So do you just stay there the whole time and work, or do you ever get to come home?" I ask.

"Mari, what's with all the questions?" Hudson squeezes my hand, chuckling.

"Just making conversation," I say, clearing my throat. My cheeks warm as I realize how bizarre my line of questioning must have seemed to Hudson, but my mind was spinning so fast with panic I didn't have time to think about how this would look.

"Hud, it's fine," Alec says. "I can come home from time to time, yes. But I prefer not to. I like to immerse myself in the culture and work as much as possible until the job's done. Sooner I'm done, sooner I can move on to the next job."

"My brother, the hustler." Audrina's words are coated in sarcasm. She folds her magazine and tosses it aside. "Mom and Dad's pride and joy."

Alec's sandy hair blows in the breeze as the

boat begins to move, and he hooks his arms around his tan legs. He's attractive. Well-educated—I assume. Hardworking. And adventurous. It's almost as if I hit the genetic lottery of sperm donors.

"Alec, I need you to ease the sheets," Duke calls into the wind, and Alec obliges.

Hudson slips his arm around me as the boat leans. I wish I could enjoy the sweet simplicity of the wind at the sails and the smell of the ocean breeze, but all I can think about is how I'm going to get Alec alone between now and Wednesday.

All I need is a minute of his time.

And then I need to hope and pray he doesn't run and tell Hudson before I get the chance.

Fuck.

Chapter Twenty-Six

Hudson

"You were all about Alec today." I'm perched on the edge of Mari's bed in her suite as she changes for bed Monday evening.

Glancing up into the dresser mirror, her eyes catch my reflection and she laughs.

"What's that supposed to mean?" she asks.

"It's like you found every little thing he said or did fascinating." I lean back, slipping my hands under my head and staring up at the walnut-stained beams that accent the vaulted ceiling. "He's not that fascinating. Trust me."

"Sensing a little jealousy over there."

Yeah.

I was fucking jealous today, and I'm not the jealous type.

"I don't get jealous," I say. "But today …

yeah … seeing you so engaged with Alec … it did something to me."

Turning, she comes to the bed, climbing in and lying down beside me. Resting on her side, she places her hand under her chin and smiles.

"That's cute," she says. "Do you think I have a crush on Alec?"

Her eyes search mine, and I hesitate. "A crush? Like a schoolyard crush?"

"I feel like you think that." Mari bites her bottom lip.

"Does it matter if I think that?"

She rolls her eyes. "Yeah, it does. Because you shouldn't care."

"You're right. I shouldn't care," I say. "But I do."

"Then stop caring."

"It's not that easy." I look away, pulling in a deep breath and letting it go. "I like spending time with you, Mari. I thought it would feel like work, like a job. But it doesn't. It's effortless. I've never had that with anyone else."

"Hudson, stop." She chuckles, rolling to her

back and folding her hands over her upper stomach.

The two of us lie in silence for a minute, staring at the ceiling, deep in thought.

"This is a job," she says a moment later. "This isn't real. It may feel real from time to time, but that's because we're good actors. It's easy to get caught up in this, but we ... just can't."

"Why not?"

"Why not?" she repeats the question as if it astounds her.

"Yeah," I say. "Why can't we get caught up in this? If it feels right, maybe it is right?"

"It's not right," she says. "A month ago, Hudson, I couldn't stand you. I literally hated your guts, and I almost spat in your coffee one morning. You're lucky Tiffin from HR walked in when she did."

I shake my head, rubbing my thumb and forefinger along my eyes.

"I probably deserved it," I say.

"You *did* deserve it." I feel her turn my way. "I'm having fun with you, Hudson. More than I thought I would. But we're not together, not in the real sense of the word. Only on paper. And for the record, I do not have a crush on Alec. I think he's nice. That's all."

I fight the pleased smile trying to claim my lips and reach for her, pulling her over my lap until she's straddling my hips.

"What are you doing?" she asks as our fingers interlace. "You're really bad at taking 'no' for an answer."

"So you're saying you don't want to be with me?" I ask. "If there was no contract and all we had was the last few weeks ..."

"Don't play the 'what if' game."

"Yes or no, Mari. Just answer the fucking question."

She rolls her eyes, biting her lower lip as she stares at the ceiling. "I don't know."

"You do know. You just don't want to say."

"I think we're having fun pretending, and we're not thinking of the reality of this," she says.

"Which is what?"

"I don't belong in your world, and I probably never will," she says, her gaze falling to

261

mine. "And I'm fine with that. I just don't think we have much in common other than enjoying each other's company."

"Isn't that the only thing that matters?" I ask.

My hands release hers before settling on her hips and sliding down her outer thighs. A thin silk camisole covers her bra-less breasts, and while I've been trying to be a perfect gentleman and not stare at the pointed buds piercing the pale fabric, I still know they're there, and my hands are aching at the thought of touching them.

"You're trying to find every excuse you can not to let yourself fall for me, Maribel," I say, my voice soft and low as my fingers graze the soft flesh of her belly. "I'm sure I could come up with a list myself if I tried, but I don't want to do that. All I want, Mari, is you."

Her expression fades, and she's still concentrating.

"I'm falling for you," I say, as if it weren't already obvious.

"You're making a big mistake." Her voice is a cracked whisper.

Sitting up, I pull her closer into my lap,

wrapping her legs around my lower back before cupping her pretty face in my hand.

"Do you want to be with me?" I ask. "Logic and rationale aside?"

I hear her swallow and watch as her tongue skims her bottom lip before she nods.

"Yes." Mari sighs.

My heart hammers in my chest as I claim her mouth, and my hands tug at the hem of her top, all but tearing it off of her.

Falling back onto the bed, she lays on my chest, sliding her hands down my stomach then farther, beneath my waistband, until she palms my throbbing cock. Sliding down my body, she unzips my shorts, freeing me and taking me in her mouth, inch by inch.

Her tongue slides around my tip before she teases the length again and again.

My body is reeling, every inch of me alive as she pleasures me.

"I knew you had a mouth on you, Mari, but fuck." I'm breathless, cock growing harder by the second.

She stops, staring up at me with a drunk-in-lust smirk before going back for more.

Mari licks and sucks and swirls until I can't take it any more, bringing me to the brink and back more times than I can stand, and when I've had enough torture, I reach for her and pull her over top of me. She giggles, pulling my shirt over my head before pressing her body against mine.

Her bare breasts are warm on my skin, and the faint scent of gardenia evaporates into the briny air around us.

Tugging at her shorts, I ease them down her hips until she rises and kicks them off. Straddling me, her wet pussy glides against my cock.

"You're all about tormenting me tonight, aren't you?" I tease.

"It's the least I could do after all the ways you tormented me the last couple of months," she says, hips circling.

"What can I say? I like being in charge."

"You think you're in charge now?" She laughs, grinding harder.

Reaching into my shorts, I retrieve my wallet and slide out a spare condom.

"You're going to fuck me," I say, voice low. "You're going to come all over my cock, and I'm going to watch."

Handing her the condom, I slip my hands behind my head and let her do the honors.

"You get off on this, don't you?" she asks, sliding the rubber down my shaft as slow as humanly fucking possible.

"I get off on beautiful women named Maribel fucking me, yes," I say.

She rises on her knees, my cock in her pretty little hand. "And what if I don't? What if I change my mind?"

"Are you thinking of not fucking me tonight?"

Mari's lips crack into a coy smile. She doesn't answer.

"Fuck me," I say. "Before that busy little brain of yours talks you out of it."

My hands grip her hips, guiding her over my cock, and she slides herself down, aided by the warm slickness of her arousal.

This woman is Novocain.

I'm numb when I'm with her, but in the best way possible.

Nothing else matters when I'm with her … the past, the future, none of it. There's a world outside that door full of obligations, heartache, and strife, but in here, it's just the two of us. Nothing more, nothing less.

Mari lowers herself again, deeper before rising on her knees and building herself to a steady rhythm. Her eyes close, and her head leans back as her hands massage her swollen breasts. They're bigger than I remember from before, but it could be the lighting or my tired eyes playing ticks on me. Either way, I'll fucking take it.

Thrusting up, I fill her with every last inch of me, watching as her mouth releases a quiet gasp and her eyes squeeze tighter.

I could do this all night with her, every night.

And after this?

I think I will.

Chapter Twenty-seven

Mari

A small golden conch shell digs into the palm of my hand Tuesday morning just after sunrise. Up ahead, a man jogs along the shore, growing closer until he comes into focus, and then I realize ...

It's Alec.

My heart quickens, and I swallow the nervous lump in my throat.

It's just the two of us on this beach—at least for now.

This is my chance.

It's now or never.

Spotting a couple more shells, I bend to pick them up, biding my time as he grows near. The sea laps across the shore, washing the sticky sand from the soles of my feet, but I feel nothing.

"Mari," he says, breathless as he stops before me. He places two fingers against his neck, his bare chest glistening with a light sheen of sweat and sea mist. "What are you doing up so early?"

"Wanted to take a walk," I say, smiling. The words are right there, on the tip of my tongue, and it's all I can do to keep from blurting them all out at once. A big string of word vomit that'll forever change this man's life.

Or maybe not.

I've tried to get to know Alec these last couple of days, and I still feel like I'm barely scratching the surface.

He seems nice. That's about all I've gathered.

"I'm going to head in, hit the shower," he says after an awkward minute of silence. "See you at breakfast?"

He gives a quick wave before jogging off toward the house, and I watch my opportunity pass me by.

"Alec, wait," I call after him, my voice carried off by a breeze.

He doesn't hear me, so I chase after him.

"Alec," I say again, louder this time.

He turns, slowing down, but he's still walking. We're maybe fifty, sixty feet from the back of the house at most.

"I have to tell you something," I say, slightly winded.

"What's up?"

He forges ahead with long strides, not stopping. The house grows closer.

There's no easy way to do this, so I decide to just put it out there. "I'm pregnant."

I expected him to stop, but he keeps walking. I don't know if he heard me.

"I'm pregnant," I say again.

We approach the back steps to the wraparound deck and he climbs them two at a time.

"Alec, say something," I say, nearly pleading.

He stops, turning to me. "Congratulations?"

"Are you asking me or telling me?"

"Is that why you and Hudson are in such a

hurry to get married?" He laughs. "God, you guys, it's not the fifties."

"The baby's yours." I cross my arms over my chest, looking away.

"Wait … what?"

Glancing up, I take a deep breath. "You know that one-night stand we had? Where you used a fake name and then deleted your Tinder profile?"

My hand moves to my lower belly, his moves to his sweaty mop of sandy blond hair.

"Fuck," he says, his eyes flicking from mine to my stomach and back. "How far along are you?"

"Almost nine weeks," I say.

He takes a step closer to me. "What are you going to do about it?"

I scoff. "What am *I* going to do about it? What? Like this is *my* problem?"

"Your body, your choice," he says, and my defensiveness ratchets down a notch. "I mean, are you going to, you know, take care of it?"

"Take care of it as in raise it? Or take care of it as in …?"

He inhales, glancing over my shoulder toward the water. Dragging his hands down his face, he turns back to me.

"I don't want to be a dad, Mari," he says. "At least not at this point in my life. And not in this way. And no offense, but not with you. You're engaged to my fucking best friend."

"Well, I'm keeping it," I say. "If you don't want to be a part of the baby's life, that's your choice."

"Don't say it like that."

"Like what?"

"Like I'm some piece of shit, deadbeat dad."

"You're certainly not father of the year."

"We used a condom," he says. "And you said you were on the pill."

"We did. And I was." I shrug. "Shit happens."

"How do you know it's mine?"

My blood heats beneath my skin. "Are you fucking serious, Alec?"

"I didn't mean it like that."

My eyes water. God damn it. Pregnancy hormones.

"You're saying all the things I hoped you weren't going to say." I wipe away a fat, soggy tear before it has the chance to roll down my ruddy, wind-burned cheeks.

His hands fall to his sides. "What did you expect me to say? Let's raise the baby like some happy fucking family and live happily ever after?"

"No!" I raise my voice. "Just … don't be a douche about it."

"Tell me what you want me to say, Mari."

"Just say you'll be there if I need you. And that you'd love to be a part of the baby's life," I say. "This baby … it's half yours. And I don't want it to grow up thinking it wasn't wanted or constantly feeling this void in his heart when he wonders why his father never came around."

"It's a boy?"

"I don't know," I scoff at him, looking away. "It's too fucking early to tell."

"I don't know anything about babies or pregnancy or any of that shit," he says.

"And you think I do?"

"I wouldn't know the first thing about how to be there for you through this, Mari."

"Just decide if you want to be involved and we can figure everything else out later," I huff. I'm so fucking annoyed with him right now. "I'm kind of taking things one day at a time anyway. I have no clue what I'm doing. And aside from my best friend, you're the only other person who knows about the baby now."

"I fucking *knew* it." The Potomac Ice Princess appears at the railing, her arms resting on the ledge as she wears a proud smirk. "I knew you were fucking pregnant. But my brother? Now that's a plot twist I didn't see coming."

She moves to the stairs, taking them one at a time as she comes closer.

"Brilliant, Mari. Really. Get my brother to knock you up, get Hudson to raise it as his," she says. "Talk about a lifetime of financial security."

"It's nothing like that," I say, lips curling into a sneer. My hand grips the railing to keep me from ripping her hair out extension by extension.

"Don't say anything to Hudson," Alec says, turning to his sister. "We're still trying to figure this

273

out."

Her mouth pulls at the sides and she lifts her hands to her lips. "Wait, what? Hudson doesn't know about this?"

Fuck, fuck, fuck.

Pushing past the two of them, I head inside to find Hudson.

I have to tell him first.

I have to tell him before Audrina does.

Chapter Twenty-eight

Hudson

I slide a chamois across the hood of my father's '64 Alfa Romeo Giulietta. It's always been my favorite of all his classic cars, something about it evoking the feel of simpler times. Timeless style. Uncommon goodness. It's flashy without being over the top, and sexy without being in-your-face.

The design is perfection.

Second to none.

This thing is freshly washed, waxed, and detailed, and as soon as I catch up with Mari, I'll see if she wants to take it for a drive. We could head into town to a little coffee shop for breakfast then I could show her some more of the sights up here.

"Hudson?" I hear her call my name from the garage entrance. "You out here?"

"Over here."

Quick footsteps pad across the concrete

toward the driveway, and she stops at the trunk of the car, like she's afraid to come closer.

"What's up?" I lean against the door, tossing the chamois over my right shoulder. Her eyes are misty, bloodshot. "God, Mari. Everything okay?"

Biting her lip, she hesitates before shaking her head. "No."

I study her face. She studies mine.

"Did something happen? Did someone hurt you?" I go to her, sliding my hands down her arms. She's cold, which makes sense. She said she was going for a walk on the beach earlier.

"I have to tell you something." Her words are steady and send a heaviness to my heart. "And before I tell you, you should know that I'm sorry. And if I could change things, I would. I'd take it back."

My stomach is tied in knots. "It has to do with Alec, doesn't it? Something happened with him? You kissed him?"

Her eyes close for a few beats, her lower lip trembling.

"I knew it. You like him," I say.

She shakes her head. "Not quite."

I half-laugh. "What do you mean, not quite?"

"I knew him before this trip," she says slowly. "We met a couple of months ago. Back in New York. We hooked up. Once. It was just a one-night thing."

I drag my hand along my jaw, brows furrowed as I listen.

"It didn't mean anything," she says. "But then ..."

"Then *what*?" I don't fucking have all day, and knowing she's about to drop some sort of bombshell on me tightens my body and shortens my fuse. "Get on with it."

"I ... somehow ... we got pregnant." Her expression freezes as she waits for my reaction, but all I feel is numb.

And it's not the good kind of numb this time.

It's the kind of numbness I've known for the better part of the last decade, the kind that turns my heart to ice and convinces my head not to give a shit about any of the women who flit in and out of my life.

"When did you know?" I ask, chest feeling as if it's about to implode.

"About a month ago?" She winces, looking up at me. "Before I signed the contract."

Blowing a breath past tight lips, I take a step back and run my fingers through my hair, tugging on the ends.

"Seriously?" I ask. "Seriously, Mari? You didn't think that maybe, just maybe you should've told me that you were fucking *pregnant* before you agreed to marry me?!"

"In my defense, you were extremely persistent, and what do you expect is going to happen when you wave five million dollars in front of a single pregnant lady?"

"So it's my fault that you lied?"

"No. It's your fault that I couldn't say no. I literally couldn't say not to that, Hudson. Who would?" she asks. "But it's my fault that I lied. And I'm sorry. And I'm telling you now."

"So Audrina was right." I huff, peering out toward the manicured hedges and shaking my head. It all makes sense now ... Mari not touching booze, her breasts getting bigger, all of it.

From the corner of my eye, I watch as Mari dabs the tears streaking down her cheek with the back of her hand. Her shoulders shake and she exhales as the two of us marinate in this new reality. Then without saying a word, she slides the diamond ring off her finger and places it gently on the trunk of my father's car before heading inside.

She's leaving.

And I'm not going to try and stop her.

Chapter Twenty-nine

Mari

I tug the zipper around my suitcase with all the strength I have. There are still five inches until it's fully closed, but this thing won't budge. It's too full.

My eyes burn and sting and tears cloud my vision, but I'm not giving up.

I've already called a cab. My things are ninety-five percent packed. I'm leaving.

The jig is up.

It's over.

Just like I expected, this entire thing exploded in our faces.

I never should've agreed. I should've gone with my gut on this and not my money-blinded brain.

Something shiny catches my eye, and as I

glance down, I realize I'm still wearing that Cartier love bracelet.

Hudson has the key.

A swift knock at the door startles my tears away temporarily, and in a flash of a second, I imagine it's Hudson, coming to talk me out of leaving. Telling me we can make it work anyway. Then I realize it's not going to happen. He didn't chase after me when I left the garage earlier, and if he didn't want me to go, he'd have stopped me by now.

"Maribel, are you in there?" It's Helena.

"Just a second," I call, running to the bathroom to splash cold water on my face. When I return, she's standing in the middle of the room, worrying her bottom lip.

"There's a cab here for you." She steps closer. "I didn't know you were leaving. Is everything all right? What happened?"

Helena's kindness hits me in the feels. I'm going to miss her hospitality, and I'm going to miss the fact that I never really got to know her as well as I'd hoped.

"The engagement is off," I say.

Her expression darkens. "What? Why? Did Hudson do something?"

I shake my head. "No. He didn't do anything."

She places her delicate hand over her chest. "I'm confused. You two seemed so happy together."

"It's a long story. Maybe Hudson can fill you in?" I peer out the window, but I can't see the circle drive from this side of the house. I muster every last reserve of strength I have and pull the suitcase zipper the rest of the way shut before forcing a meek smile. "I probably shouldn't keep the cab waiting. I'm sure the meter's running."

Yanking the suitcase off the bed, I wheel it to the door. I'm leaving several things here. Shoes, purses, Chanel dresses that have no business hanging in some closet in Orchard Hill, Nebraska …

"Sweetheart," Helena says, following me. She places her hand on my back, but I can't bear to turn around and look at her. "I have no idea what's going on with you two, but whatever it is, it can be fixed. And if it can't be fixed, well, we can always sweep it under the rug." She chuckles softly. "Regardless, all I know is that you make my son happy. Happier than I've seen him in years. After Audrina broke his heart in college, I didn't think he'd ever be the same after that. And he wasn't. She ruined him. She broke his spirit. Until you."

Turning to face her, I have to know. "Audrina ... broke up with him?"

Helena nods. "Yes. They dated all through college. Very seriously. They were going to get married, until she cheated on him with one of his best friends. After that, he was hell bent on getting back at her any way he could. I have to admit, as shocked as I was when I found out he was marrying you, all I could think was that I was glad he wouldn't be marrying her. I know she's Cybil's daughter and all, but she doesn't deserve my son. Not after what she did to him."

"Wait." I can't breathe. The room tilts and spins as I wrap my head around this. "So you never expected him to marry her?"

Her face twists in confusion. "What are you talking about, dear?"

He lied.

Hudson lied.

He lied to me from the very beginning.

There was no arranged marriage bullet he was trying to dodge.

He wanted revenge.

He wanted to hurt Audrina.

And he used me to do it.

My chest stings more than I thought it would. There may as well be an arrow piercing my heart. I liked him. I really did.

And to think, for a minute there, I almost believed this fake little arrangement was turning into something real.

Chapter Thirty

Hudson

"What's this I hear about Mari leaving?" Cybil breaks the awkward silence at the lunch table. "That can't be true. She's been having a ball since she got here."

No one answers.

The clink of glassware and silver fills the silence.

I stare at the steaming bowl of seafood chowder before me, unable to touch it, my fist clenched hard around my spoon.

"Is she okay?" Cybil won't drop it, but I'm not surprised. She's nosier than she is compassionate. "Did she have a family emergency?"

Audrina sighs. "Hudson found out that Alec knocked Mari up."

A hush falls over the table.

Alec chokes on his ice water.

"Audrina," Cybil scolds her with her name. "It's not nice to make things up."

"It's the truth." Audrina smirks. "I knew she was hiding something. Nobody would listen to me. You were all Maribel this and Maribel that, like she was the second coming of Christ."

"Audrina." Duke coughs her name. "That's enough."

"God, I'm so sick of you people and your delusions." Her voice escalates. "And I'm tired of no one ever listening to me."

"Hudson, is this true?" My mother bats her eyes at me, and the entire table stares in my direction.

I drop my spoon, pushing my chair away from the table and tossing my unused napkin over my untouched soup before bolting for the door.

I need air.

I need to get away from these people.

Slamming the sliding door behind me, I move to the corner of the deck farthest away from the dining room. Resting my hands on the railing, I close my eyes and take a deep breath.

Mari left an hour ago, and I feel her absence in every part of me. More than I expected to. More than I thought I would.

The sound of the door sliding open and shut pulls me out of my moment.

"When are you going to realize I'm the only woman that's ever going to be right for you?" Audrina's voice is nails on a chalkboard. I refuse to look at her. "We were young back then, Hudson. We were just kids. I made a mistake. A horrible, selfish mistake. But I never stopped loving you. And you never stopped loving me."

"Wrong," I say, teeth gritting. "I stopped loving you the day I walked in on you fucking my best friend in our bed."

"I've told you a million times, I wish I could go back and change that, but I can't." She whines like a demanding little toddler when she speaks, causing my grip to squeeze the railing harder.

"Go away, Audrina."

"Not until you look at me."

I shake my head once, jaw clenched as I watch the waves. Normally I find peace in them, but today they're particularly tumultuous.

"Because of you," I say, lock-jawed. "I haven't been able to trust anyone else. I haven't been able to love anyone else. I've spent almost an entire decade cheating myself out of the kind of happiness I deserved." Finally, I face her. "Now get out of my fucking face, you avaricious little whore."

Audrina freezes, jaw locked open.

"Go." My voice booms, startling her into finally getting the fuck out of my face just as Alec comes outside. She pushes past him, running away in tears.

I don't give a fuck.

"Hey, man." Alec jams his hands into his pockets. "I just wanted to say, I had no idea. And I hope you guys didn't break up because of me."

I don't say anything. It isn't his fault. And I'm not upset with *him*.

I'm upset with the circumstances.

And I'm upset that I was so close to tasting love and the kind of emancipation my soul had been craving all these years … only to watch it disintegrate overnight.

"Don't worry about us," I say, placing my hand on his shoulder. "Our issues have nothing to do with you."

At least not in a way he'd understand ...

"You going to do the right thing? You going to take care of them?" I ask. Regardless of my frustration with the fact that she completely withheld the pregnancy from me, I do want to see to it that she'll be properly cared for.

Alec chuckles. "I don't want to be a father, are you kidding me?"

"You don't have a choice. She's having your child."

He leans closer, like he's going to tell me a secret. "Hud, I tried telling her to, you know, get rid of it earlier, and she flipped out on me. So then I just told her what she wanted to hear so she'd calm down."

My skin heats. I'm on fire. "You have to help her, Alec. She has nothing."

"She'll figure it out. Can't she get on government aid or something?"

"So she's not your problem? Is that what you're saying?"

"Hud, calm down." He titters. "She'll be fine."

"And you know that … how?"

"She's a smart girl. She'll land on her feet. Girls like her always do." Alec slicks his hand through his hair, his eyes darting anywhere but in my direction. I'm making him nervous, and rightfully so. I've known this guy my entire life, and I've never known him to maintain a single responsibility that wasn't self-serving.

His attitude is disappointing but expected.

"If you're not going to help her, tell her now," I say. "Tell her before she gets to the end of her pregnancy and realizes you're not going to be there and you never were planning to in the first place"

He's quiet, and I hope to God he's letting my thoughts sink in, but it's hard telling with him.

"Do the right thing, Alec." I punch his shoulder before storming away. "You only get one chance to make it right. After that, you're fucked."

I need to get the hell out of Montauk and back to the city, to my office, to the routine that's helped me through the last decade of my existence.

I'm done here.

Chapter Thirty-one

Mari

"Sweetheart, what are you doing here? I had no idea you were coming home." My mother cups my face in her hands, welcoming me inside the foyer of our family's home.

My shoulders tremble, and I try my hardest to keep myself together, but my legs are shaky and my eyelids heavy and I just want to lie in my childhood bed and forget about life for a while.

"You look like you've been crying." She inspects my face. "What aren't you telling me? Did something happen with Hudson?"

She pulls my left hand toward her, searching for my engagement ring.

"The bastard left you, didn't he?" she asks, lips pressed flat.

I shake my head. "I left him."

Her expression shifts, her mouth agape.

"Why?"

"First he was a bastard. Now he's wonderful?" I half-laugh, half give up.

"Come inside. I'll have your father carry your bags upstairs when he gets home. I have to say, we're thrilled you're home, but I'm sorry you had to come home under these circumstances." She leads me up the split foyer, toward the living room, and covers me with a knit blanket the second I spread out across the sofa.

I don't move for a minute.

I simply breathe in the comforting cocktail of scents that make up this house. My mother's pot roast in the slow cooker. Her favorite cotton-clean fabric softener. A black cherry candle flickering on the stove.

Across the room my mother rocks in her La-Z-Boy, worry lines sprouting across her forehead as she twirls a strand of gray-blonde hair around her finger. She doesn't say anything, but she doesn't have to. I know she'll listen when I'm ready to talk.

Lying on my back with my hands folded over my stomach, I stare at the ceiling and take a deep breath.

"I'm pregnant," I say, exhaling.

My mother stops rocking, stops twirling her hair.

"And it's not Hudson's. It's this guy I met a couple months ago and it was a fling that meant absolutely nothing," I continue. "But the guy happened to be a friend of Hudson's because of course he was."

I squeeze my eyes, this feels like the hardest confession of all if only because I've never lied to my parents before, not like this.

"And Hudson? He was my boss in New York," I say. "The one I hated. The one who treated me like shit all the time."

My mom still hasn't said a word, still hasn't moved. That's never a good sign.

"He needed a fake fiancée," I say. "And I said yes because he was going to pay me a lot of money. Like, a lot. And I knew I was pregnant. I knew I'd need a way to support myself and the baby. And he wouldn't take no for an answer."

I run my fingers through my hair before digging them into my scalp. It feels good to feel something other than dazed and disoriented. I left Montauk yesterday, cabbed it back to the city, slept on Isabelle's couch for a night, then grabbed the

294

first flight to Omaha the next day.

The last twenty-four hours has been a blur and a nightmare all rolled into one, and though I knew this day was inevitable in some ways, it still doesn't feel real.

"Anyway, I came clean to Hudson about the pregnancy," I say. "And he was upset. Understandably. So I left. But as I was leaving, his mom said something to me that made me realize that he lied to me about something too. Something pretty major. So I guess you could say we're even now. But we're also over. And that's that." I look at her across the room. She's biting her nail now. At least she moved. "And now I'm home ... homeless and pregnant. Yay."

She stares at me, hard.

"Mom, say something. You're freaking me out." I sit up, throwing the blanket off me because suddenly I'm hotter than a furnace.

"I ... wow, Mari." She sits up in her chair, clearly at a loss for words. "I don't know what to say other than we'll get through this. You've got us. Daddy and me. And we'll make the best of this situation."

She gets up, taking a seat beside me and

placing her arm around my shoulders. I stare straight ahead, but I feel her looking at me. A moment later, she kisses the side of my head.

"Life has a way of forcing us to go exactly in the direction we're supposed to go, even when we don't want to," she says. "You may not think so now, but someday you'll look back and you'll connect the dots and it'll all have been worth it."

The sliding glass door to the patio fills our quiet house.

"Mari, what are you doing home?" My father asks when he comes around the corner. He takes one look at me and silences his commentary.

With tear-filled eyes, I hold my wrist out, the one with the Cartier bracelet. "Think you have any tools that could get this stupid thing off me?"

"Damn right, I do."

Chapter Thirty-two

Hudson

"Mr. Rutherford." Shoshannah rises at her desk the second she sees me. "You're back early. I thought you were out of the office until the end of June?"

"Yes, well, it appears as though I'm back now. Doesn't it, Savannah?" I grab the stack of mail at the edge of her desk, which doesn't appear to have been sorted, then I toss it back toward her. "Sort this, please, Savannah. We're not fucking animals."

"Y-yes. S-sorry." She scrambles to grab the mish-mash of envelopes on her desk, lowering herself to her knees to grab the ones that fell to the floor.

Up ahead, I see Tiffin from HR peek her head out her door before clambering back to her desk. I'm sure they're all IM-ing each other with the news. They think they're so clever, using instant messaging to cover their tracks, but the joke's on them. I don't give a flying fuck if they love me or hate me.

They're sheep. Their opinions don't matter.

Unlocking my office door, I burst through and slam it behind me. Dropping my briefcase on one of the guest chairs, I fire up my computer and prepare to catch up on emails.

I need to lose myself in work.

I need to get so fixated and focused on numbers and lines and parametrics that the goings-on of the last twenty-four hours don't fucking matter.

An hour passes.

Then another, and another.

By the time I've caught myself up and responded to the senders of most importance, I tend to the desktop of my computer, where I'd saved the draft for Abel's shed just weeks ago. Covering my mouth with my hand, I pull in a hard breath, release it, then drag the shed to the trash folder.

I already sent him the design, but I have a feeling we won't be discussing revisions anytime soon.

***

"Mr. Rutherford." Marta startles the second I enter my apartment that evening after work, dropping a cleaning rag at her feet. With being gone, I'd reduced her shift to half days while keeping her full-time pay. My treat to her for a job always well done. I was home this morning, and I should have left a note, but my mind was elsewhere. "I didn't expect to see you. You scared me."

"Sorry, Marta." I step into the kitchen, sitting my briefcase on the counter.

"Back so soon?"

"I had to cut my vacation short." I yank the fridge door open, staring at the empty, sparkling clean shelves. Makes sense. No point in keeping a stocked kitchen when the man of the house is supposed to be gone for a month.

Pizza it is.

"Where's Ms. Collins?" Marta asks, glancing around like she expects to see her hiding behind the fiddle leaf fig tree in the corner.

"We've ended our arrangement."

"I'm sorry to hear it didn't work out, sir."

Crossing my arms, I ask, "Be honest with me, Marta. Did you know Mari was pregnant?"

Marta's dark eyes widen. "I did not. I take it the baby … is not yours?"

Pressing my lips flat, I say, "No, Marta. The baby isn't mine."

Her gaze darts around, like she has something she needs to get off her chest, but she's afraid to say it.

"What?" I ask. "What do you want to say?"

"I'd rather not."

"You can tell me," I say. "It's not like I'm going to fire you for being honest." I huff, shaking my head. "There aren't enough honest people in this world, Marta. Everyone's got something to hide and something to gain by hiding it."

Including … even myself.

In my heart of hearts, I know it's not right to be so upset with her when I wasn't exactly forthcoming when we made our little arrangement.

But a baby is a game changer.

You can hide feelings. You can hide your intent. You can't hide a baby.

"You want my honest opinion, Mr. Rutherford?" Marta lifts a dark brow, taking a hesitant step toward me.

I give her my full, focused attention.

"I think it was wrong of you to put her in that position. To make her an offer no woman in their right mind would've refused," she says, choosing her words carefully. "Regardless of her personal circumstances, you knew she needed money and you took advantage of that." Exhaling, she places her hand over her heart. "Oh, goodness. That was a bit harsh of me, wasn't it?"

I keep my expression blank, but I shake my head. "No, Marta. I needed to hear that."

"She was a nice girl," she says. "But I have to admit, I purposely kept my distance from her. I didn't want to get close. I didn't want to get attached. I've learned over the years to keep my distance from all the women you bring home because they're never going to be around for very long. It's easier to keep back and be cordial. They probably think I'm a bit cold, but it's the way it has to be."

"God, this situation is so fucked." I bury my face in my palms, rubbing my eyes and groaning. "Maybe I have no right to be mad at her."

"Maybe." Marta smirks.

"And the guy who knocked her up? He has no intention of helping her. He's just going to bail on her."

Marta clucks her tongue in disapproval. "Shame."

"She's alone," I say. "And homeless because I moved her out of her apartment. She has nothing. I'm sure she went home. To Nebraska. I can't imagine she has anywhere else to go."

"You should call her, sir."

"Yeah," I say. "I should."

Chapter Thirty-three

Mari

"Oh, my goodness, Maribel, look at this!" My mother holds up a lamb onesie and squeals.

"It's way too early to be buying that stuff," I say, yanking it out of her hand and placing it back on the rack. We came to Target for five things and somehow we ended up with an overflowing cart of random shit, and now we're in the baby clothes section. "I'm not even out of the first trimester."

"Don't be so negative. I'm only trying to make lemonade out of these lemons," she says, swatting her hand at me. "Not that the baby's a lemon. But you know what I mean. I'm trying to make this fun, Mar. Work with me here."

She plucks a miniature three-piece suit from one rack and a lavender polka dot dress from another, holding them up.

"Do you think it's a boy or a girl?" she asks.

"I don't know?"

"I knew from the very beginning with you," she says, grinning as her eyes flash with bittersweet nostalgia. "Mother's instinct. You were the easiest pregnancy. And the best baby. I'd give anything to relieve some of those moments. Cherish them. It goes so fast, trust me."

She points at me before placing the clothes back on their respective hooks and moving onto a haphazard clearance rack that looks like a pack of wild monkeys tore through it.

My bag vibrates, and it takes a second for me to realize someone's calling me. For a moment, I consider letting it go to voicemail. I'm not in the mood to talk to anyone, and my mother is still yammering on about how easy I was to potty-train and how I never once tried to climb out of my crib.

But curiosity gets the better of me, and I reach in to check the Caller ID.

Hudson's name is the last thing I expect to see flashing on the screen, but there it is in bold white letters.

Struggling to breathe for a second, it's as if time freezes.

He hasn't reached out to me since I left Montauk earlier this week. Not once.

What could he possibly want now?

Before I so much as consider answering it, I force myself to press the red button on the screen. I can't talk to him. Not today.

Not ever.

Chapter Thirty-four

Hudson

The call goes to voicemail, just as I suspected it would.

"Attention Airstream Passengers, Flight 607 from New York to Omaha's Eppley Airfield will begin boarding momentarily. Please report to Terminal C at this time," a woman's voice plays over the speakers.

Checking my seat assignment, I move toward the line beginning to form outside the door to the jet bridge.

Ten minutes later, I'm settling into my first class window seat, paging through an in-flight magazine filled with all kinds of fascinating junk everyone wants but no one will ever use. The woman in the aisle across from me begins to power down her cell phone, and I figure I may as well follow suit. We'll be airborne soon anyway.

Grabbing my phone from my pocket, I hover

over the power button before opting to send a quick text to Mari.

I'M SORRY I LET YOU GO.

I wait a moment, but she doesn't respond.

It doesn't matter anyway.

I'll see her soon enough.

Chapter Thirty-five

Mari

"You did the right thing." Isabelle sighs into the phone. "Don't beat yourself up about it, okay?"

"I'm trying not to. I was so sure of everything until he called. And then he sent that text." I roll to my side, pulling my covers up to my shoulders. It's only two o'clock in the afternoon but I'm already gearing up for a hibernation-worthy nap.

"Of course he's sorry he let you go," she says. "He knows he doesn't deserve you and now he's going to try to get you back. It's cool and all that he's over the pregnancy thing, but it doesn't change the fact that he lied to you. He got you to sign a contract under false pretenses. I'm not even sure that's legal."

I groan into my pillow. "Isabelle, I don't even know what to do anymore. Or what to think. All I know is I knew better. I damn. Well. Knew better."

"Hey, I was thinking I'd come out and see you next month?" she changes the subject. She's good at doing that when my self-loathing grows too tiresome.

"I don't want to subject you to that," I say. "You'd be bored out of your mind here. I wouldn't do that to you."

"But at least I'd be bored with you," she says, and I can almost hear the sweet smile in her voice. "I miss my best friend. Like crazy."

"Me too."

"I'll look at flights as soon as we hang up."

"Awesome." I yawn. "I'm taking a nap as soon as we hang up."

Isabelle laughs. "Good for you, Mama. Get that shut eye while you still can."

Hanging up, I reach toward the Target bag on the floor. My mom insisted on buying a gender neutral lamb onesie. She said it would help me get excited about this whole baby thing and forget about Hudson for a while. I kind of feel like her logic is a little faulty there, but it is freaking adorable.

I run my fingers over the fuzzy lamb wool

and the cashmere soft fabric before bringing it to my cheek. Eyes closed, I drift away, seeking temporary refuge from the shit storm that has become my life.

Chapter Thirty-six

Hudson

I don't expect to be greeted with open arms—or a smile for that matter. But the look on Abel's face when he opens the door sends a chill down my spine.

"Hudson." He steps outside, pulling the front door closed behind him. "What are you doing here?"

"I need to speak to Mari."

His arms fold across his barrel chest. "I'm sorry. I can't allow that."

I half-chuckle. "You can't allow that? She's a grown woman. I wanted to apologize to her in person. I came all this way because that's how much she means to me."

"I'm sorry, Hudson. I'm sure she means a lot to you, but she's my daughter, and she means a lot to me too," he says. "You broke your promise to me. You said you wouldn't hurt her, but you did.

For that reason alone, I can't let you see her. Plus, you lied to me. You came here saying you were in love with my daughter and you wanted to marry her. Turns out you were just using her."

"I respect your feelings, Abel, and you're not incorrect. You have every reason to despise me and everything about me," I say. "But please, if I could just see her for a minute. I just want to apologize, and then I'll never bother her again."

Abel's mouth forms a hard line and he pushes an impatient breath through his bulbous nose.

"Look," I say. "I've never been good at taking 'no' for an answer, and that's what got the two of us into this mess in the first place. I'm trying to make things right."

"I appreciate persistence, Hudson." Abel cocks his head. "But I've got a hell of a lot more of it than you. I can go all night with you if you want, but I'm still not letting you see my daughter. Now, stop wasting my time and yours. Go back to the city where you belong. We don't share your values. Not here."

"Fair enough." I sigh, never feeling so defeated in my life. "Can you just tell her I'm not mad at her, and I never had a right to be?"

He says nothing, but the answer resides in his cold, unfeeling gaze.

Turning to leave, I climb back into my rental car and pull out of the Collins' driveway, heading north up the hill we once walked together one balmy spring night.

Passing the Queen Anne and the European Romantic that Mari used to pretend was her castle as a child, I turn the corner and spot a dilapidated Frank Lloyd Wright prairie-style house with a bright red FOR SALE sign in the front yard.

It's a shame anyone let this masterpiece fall apart like this.

And I can't, in good faith, leave this historical piece of art to disintegrate even further.

Pulling into the weeded driveway, I take my phone from my pocket. Before I realize what I'm doing, I've dialed the number on the sign.

"Alexa Lowell speaking, First Class Realty," she says.

Chapter Thirty-seven

Mari

"You're getting good at these." My mom's friend, Terri, sips the turtle mocha I whipped up a minute ago and pats my shoulder. "Well done. I'll be in the office if you need anything. You and Jaime have the front, right? Morning rush should be over."

I've been home a week and already my parents lined me up with a job. This is like college all over again, but I'm grateful to have something keeping me busy. Moping around the house and ruminating on everything is only making me feel a thousand times shittier.

The bells on the door jangle and a woman walks in. Jaime calls her by name and asks if she wants "the usual."

A couple of guys from the phone company walk in next, so I hit the register to take their orders while Jaime fusses with the cappuccino machine.

"Small coffee," the first one says. "One cream. Two sugars."

I ring him up and he takes his change, sparing none for the clearly marked tip jar mere inches from him. The second guy orders a large coffee with two shots of espresso, no cream or sugar, and tips two dollars. Just eyeballing the tip jar, I think we're at somewhere around fifteen bucks for tips, and we've been open the last four hours. At this rate, I might be able to buy myself a half tank of gas by tomorrow.

The second man steps away. I'm seconds from grabbing their drinks when I realize there's a third man. I didn't see him come in with them, and I must not have heard the bells on the door, but he's there.

Standing right in front of me.

"Hudson," I say, feeling the hot flush of my face in real time. I walk away from the cash register and up to Jaime. "I'm sorry. I'm so sorry. I have to deal with something really quick. Can you get the other two orders?"

Jaime's eyes glide over my shoulders toward Hudson. "You okay?"

"Yeah, yeah. Just give me a minute." I storm

from around the counter and pull him toward the back of the shop. "Stalking is illegal in all fifty states. Including Nebraska."

He smirks. "I literally had no idea you worked here. I'm just as shocked as you are."

Frowning, I say, "Seriously, Hudson? Or is that just another one of your lies?"

"What are you talking about?"

"I know," I say, arms folded. "I know all about Audrina. How you wanted to get back at her. And how you used me to do it."

His smirk fades.

"Yeah," I say. "That's what I thought."

"I was going to tell you," he says. "I came to your house last week. Your dad wouldn't let me in."

"You did?"

"Yep. He didn't tell you?"

"No," I say.

"I didn't expect him to," Hudson says. "But I was there. And I fought like hell, but your dad is pretty fucking persistent."

"That he is." I don't let it show, but I'm slightly disappointed that my father kept that from me. Not that I'd have wanted to see Hudson, but it would've been nice to know that he flew all the way here just to see me. "Have you been here all this time?"

He shakes his head. "I put an offer on a house last week. Came here today to finish the deal and take possession."

"You bought a house? In Orchard Hills?"

"I'm restoring a Frank Lloyd Wright house. It's on that street you liked, the one with all the big houses," he says.

I know the house he's talking about.

"The Arthur Feuerstein house," I say.

"Yeah," he says. "That's the one. I'm restoring it, and then when I'm finished, I'll probably donate it to the local historical society if I can't find a buyer who'll appreciate what it means to live in a literal work of art."

"How noble of you."

"I don't expect you to understand how deep my passion for architecture runs," he says. "But the mocking is completely unnecessary."

317

"How long are you going to be here fixing it up? And what about the firm back in New York?" It's weird asking him questions like we're on good terms. Nothing has changed. I'm nothing more than curious.

"Six months, give or take?" he says. "And I'm going to divide my time. Every other week until the house is finished."

Placing my hands on my hips, I decide to get back to business. Lifting my head high, I say, "Okay, well, I'd appreciate it if you'd stay out of my way while you're in town and I'll stay out of yours."

"Mari."

Another customer, an older woman, enters the shop. So much for the end of the morning rush.

"I was hoping we could still talk sometime," he says, his eyes drinking me in like it could be the last time.

"There's nothing left to talk about, Hudson." I look to the lady, watching her huff at the counter. Jaime's still working on drinks for the guys. "I have to get back to work."

"You're angry with me," he says. "I get that. And you should be. You're right—I misled you.

And you can be as angry as you need to be. But you should know I'm sorry. For whatever it's worth, I'm sorry."

With that, he turns and leaves. My chest tightens.

I want to scream.

I want to cry.

I want to run to him.

I want to kiss him.

I want to slap him.

But I can't do any of that, so I force a smile on my face and greet the silver-haired lady shooting daggers my way.

Chapter Thirty-eight

Hudson

"I think we could have the roof done for you by the middle of next week." A contractor in a faded green t-shirt removes his Royals cap and scratches his brow, squinting toward the house.

"I'd like the estimate in writing by noon tomorrow."

"Yeah, we can do that."

Scanning the expansive property, I make a mental note to get an estimate on landscaping next time I'm here. The hedges are overgrown, there's a dying linden tree in the back yard, and the lawn is peppered with crab grass. This thing's going to be a sight for sore eyes by the time I'm finished.

About a block away, a woman in black leggings, electric green sneakers, and a neon blue t-shirt strides up the other side of the street, arms swinging and white earbuds dangling down the sides of her face. The closer she gets, the more I'm certain it's Mari.

"Sorry. Will you excuse me?" I say to the contractor, stepping toward the edge of my yard.

Yep.

It's her.

She isn't looking in my direction. At all. And clearly she has no plans to stop and chat.

"Mari," I call to her as I cross the street.

She glances at me for half a second before redirecting her attention ahead. She doesn't stop.

"Mari, wait." I pick up my pace, watching as her shoulders slump and she finally slows to a stop.

Turning on her heel, she yanks her earbuds and places her hands on her hips.

"Yeah?" she asks.

"What are you doing?"

"Taking a walk …"

Our eyes meet, and my stomach twists. Her thick blonde hair is pulled back from her face with the help of an elastic headband, and her blue eyes flash deep and stormy.

I hurt her.

And I hurt her because she liked me.

And she's still hurting because she still likes me.

"Interesting route," I say.

Mari rolls her eyes. "You literally bought a house a block away from my parents. Believe me, this isn't intentional or I'd have stopped and said hi."

"How long are you going to punish me?" I ask.

She glances away, sighing, and then her eyes flick up to mine. "*Punish* you?"

"I'm going back to the city tomorrow," I say. "I'd love to spend a little time with you tonight. We've got a lot to discuss."

"Like how you lied to me?"

"I'd like a chance to explain."

"No, you just want a chance to justify what you did," she says. "Regardless, I lied to you. You lied to me. The relationship was fake. And now it's over."

"You're oversimplifying it."

"Am I?" Mari scoffs, dragging her sneaker across the pitted concrete sidewalk before shaking her head and staring into the distance.

"I'm going back to the city tomorrow," I say. "I'll be back a week after that. Maybe you need some time. Some space. If you change your mind and you want to talk, I'll be here."

She says nothing.

"Even if you don't want to admit it, Mari, there was something there. I felt it. I know you did too," I say, moving closer. "If I didn't believe in the possibility of something amazing, I wouldn't be standing here, fighting for it. Fighting for *us*."

"How noble of you." She lifts her earbuds and begins to drown me out. She's heard enough. "Bye, Hudson."

Chapter Thirty-nine

Mari

"Buy a vowel!" My dad shouts at the TV, as if the Wheel of Fortune contestants can hear him. "We need vowels. Come on, people."

"No," Mom says. "He needs to pick an 'r.' Why hasn't anyone picked 'r' yet?"

The contestant lands on $600 and chooses 's' and Vanna strolls across the stage in a glimmering gold gown, tapping four letters as they illuminate.

A blessing in disguise.

I could solve the puzzle now, but I don't want to ruin it for my parents. They live for this. In fact, there's a small steno book in the top drawer of the coffee table where they've been tallying who guesses the puzzles correctly the most. Last I knew, my mom is up by seven.

"Now what in the world could that be?" Mom leans forward in her chair, as if being a few extra inches closer to the screen could possibly help her.

My dad drags his hand along his bristled jaw, eyes squinting.

Turning my attention to my phone, I take a quiet picture of the TV screen and text it to Isabelle with the caption, "JUST WANTED TO SHOW YOU WHAT YOU'RE MISSING OUT ON HERE."

She responds immediately with an emoji that's both laughing and crying, and then the screen turns black and my phone begins to buzz with an incoming call. It's a weird number, one I've never seen before. It looks foreign, and I almost decide not to answer it, but my curiosity gets the better of me.

Sitting up, I clear my throat and press the green button. "Hello?"

The line is quiet for a second, and I pull the phone from my ear to make sure I'm still connected.

"Hello?" I ask again.

"Mari?" A guy's voice says my name.

"Who is this?" My parents are both staring at me now, but I wave them off and tell them it's okay. Rising, I leave the living room and stroll down the hall to my room, closing the door behind me.

"It's Alec."

I stop in my tracks. Until now, I hadn't thought about him at all. I'd actually written him off, opting to fill myself with realistic expectations rather than sit around and hope for a miracle that was never going to happen.

"Hi." I perch myself on the side of my bed, drawing my knees to my chest. It won't be long until I won't be able to sit like this anymore.

"How are you?" he asks. "How are you feeling? How's the baby?"

"Good." I speak slow and carefully, my inquisitiveness at an all-time peak. "Everything's good. What's ... going on?"

"I'm in Hong Kong," he says. "Just woke up actually. Didn't sleep much last night. Haven't slept that well since I got here, honestly."

"Oh. Um. I'm ... sorry?"

"Ever since you told me about the baby, I've just been thinking about it." I hear him exhale on the other end, his voice muffled for a moment before the swish of covers fills the receiver. I picture him on the other side of the world, pacing his hotel room. "I feel bad about what I said to you—about asking you to, you know, take care of it. That was cold. I was in shock. That's no excuse, but anyway, I wanted you to know that I want to be there for you any way I can. Financially or otherwise. I'm sure there's a lot to work out. Scheduling. Co-parenting. That sort of thing. I don't know. We'll figure it out. I mean, if that's okay with you? Maybe you don't even want me to be a part of this?"

"Alec." I clear my throat, feeling my lips pull at the corners. I've never felt so relieved in my life. "I would love for you to be a part of the baby's life, and I would appreciate any help you could give me."

He exhales. "Oh, good. Thank God. I figured you probably hated me after what I said to you. I was actually prepared for you to hang up on me."

"No, no. I wouldn't do that." I slide back on the bed, pressing my back against the headboard. A weightless calm washes over me, like the feeling that everything's probably going to be all right.

"I'm supposed to be in Hong Kong for the

next six months," he says. "But I was thinking maybe I'd come back sometime in the next week or two so we could talk about everything in person?"

"I'm in Nebraska," I say. "Just so you know, I'm not in the city anymore. But you're welcome to come here. I imagine my parents might want to meet you, you know, since we're going to be family."

God, it's so weird to think of it like that.

Alec Sheffield, my Tinder hook up, is going to be family.

I place my hand on my lower belly, grateful that this tiny life won't have to grow up without a father.

"That's fine," he says. "We'll figure this out together, Mari. I'm really sorry."

"Don't be. We both got ourselves in this situation. It's no more your fault than it is mine."

"I'll text you once I book my flight. I've got to hit the shower and head to the office." His words are lighter, airier now.

"See you soon, Alec."

Chapter Forty

Hudson

Main Street in Orchard Hills leaves much to be desired as far as lunch options are concerned, but I've narrowed it down to a deli and a Thai place that both happen to straddle the coffee shop where Mari works.

Climbing out of my rental truck, I lock the doors and head up the sidewalk toward the deli. Unable to resist, I nonchalantly glance inside the coffee place, curious to see if she's behind the counter today.

Only she's not.

She's seated at a table on the other side of the window, sipping on tea and smiling as she locks eyes with some guy. My heart drops. Someone may as well have punched me in the chest.

She's laughing, nodding. Her head tilts and her fingers trace the rim of her mug. There's something relaxed about her, genuinely happy.

Liquid heat scorches through my veins and my jaw clenches.

He's probably some old high school boyfriend who suddenly feels the need to sweep her off her feet and be her knight in shining armor now that she's back in town.

I refuse to allow this.

Before I've had a chance to calm down or rationally talk myself out of it, I'm blazing through the front door of the shop and charging at the two of them.

"Who the hell is this?" I ask when I approach, like I have any right to that answer.

Her cheerful expression fades into a scowl and she rises. "Hudson, what are you doing?"

The man across from her turns to face me, but it isn't some high school boyfriend or local idiot asshole.

"Alec?" I ask, glaring.

"Hudson." He stands, smiling and leaning in to give me a hug. He's happy to see me, but he doesn't get it. Retracting his reach, he takes a seat again. I can't look at him. Seeing how happy Mari was with him makes me want to knock his fucking block off, and I've never hit a man in my life. It's not my style. "Whoa. Wasn't expecting to see you here. You two back together?"

"No," Mari informs him immediately. "We're not. He bought a house here. *In my hometown.*" She emphasizes the last bit of detail as if it fucking matters at this point.

My vision blurs as it passes between the two of them, and for a moment, I think about Audrina and how she'd been screwing my best friend behind my back for months and I hadn't the slightest idea.

I know Mari's not mine — at least not any more, but the idea of her and Alec hitting it off ... the idea that she might want him over me ... fucking kills me.

"Alec came so we could discuss our future," Mari says.

"Your future?" I ask, teeth gritting. A couple of weeks ago, he was telling her to get rid of the baby because he didn't want to be a father.

"The future as it pertains to our situation," she clarifies.

"What, now you want to be some fucking stand up guy?" I spit my words at him. "Now you want to come in and save the day?"

"Hudson, what's this about?" Alec scratches at his temple. "I'm doing the right thing. I'm doing what *you* told me to do. I mean, I'm doing it because I want to, but I thought about what you said." I feel Mari's stare land on me, but my glare is locked on him. "I'm going to take care of her. Of the baby. That upsets you, why?"

Because I wanted to be there for her.

Because maybe deep down, a small part of me wishes it were my baby she was carrying.

The two of them will forever have this connection, and she deserves better.

No doubt Alec has good intentions, but I've known him my entire life. He's all talk and no follow-through. I can only hope it'll be different now that his unborn child is involved.

Turning to Mari, I see the hope in her eyes, the relief in her demeanor. I don't want to take that away from her.

"Forget it." My shoulders tighten, and I check my watch. I need to grab lunch and get back to the house. The demo crew tore down the old plaster walls last week, and I've got an electrical crew coming at one-thirty to get started on bringing everything to code.

I leave.

I walk away, leaving Mari in Alec's hands.

It fucking kills me, and if he so much as lets her down once, I'm going to kill him.

Chapter Forty-one

Mari

"Do you need a place to stay while you're in town, Alec?" My mother pours him a cup of Folgers coffee. "You're welcome to stay with us or we can make some hotel recommendations. There's a Super 8 just off the highway that's been recently remodeled. I hear good things. Has a pool and a fitness center."

"Mom, he's fine." I chuckle. She's going overboard with the hospitality today, treating Alec like the visiting King of England.

"So, Alec, you're a marketing guy?" Dad asks, crossing his legs wide at the head of the table. "You come up with any jingles or anything like that?"

Alec fights a smile, shaking his head. "I do online marketing. Social media presence. Brand building. Search-engine optimization. That sort of thing."

"I've been thinking about getting one of this Insta-macallits for my company. I've got a Facebook page. Think we've got about three hundred likes so far? I don't post anything on there. I wouldn't even know what to say." Dad takes a sip of the coffee Mom places in front of him. "What do you say? I've never understood those websites anyway. Who cares what I ate for breakfast or what movie I saw last night. Why does everyone need to tell everyone what they're doing all the damn time?"

Alec laughs. "It's a bit more complex than that. If we had more time, I'd outline a quick strategy for you. Maybe once I get back to Hong Kong I can send you some notes?"

"Yeah. I'd like that." Dad nods.

Mom takes a seat next to Alec, resting her chin in her hand as she stares at him. I can tell he notices, but he's trying to be polite. I'd kick her under the table if I could. She needs to stop.

"I wonder whose eyes the baby will have," Mom muses out loud. "Alec, you have dimples, right?"

"Mom." I clear my throat.

"I'm sorry. I'm just excited. Didn't think I'd

get to be a grandma so young," she says. "How do your parents feel about this? Will this be their first?"

Alec nods. "Yeah, we haven't really discussed it yet. They know about it. Thanks to my sister. But we haven't had a chance to really sit down."

My dad frowns. "Oh?"

"So you're working in Hong Kong," Mom says. "What are you going to do if she goes into labor?"

He glances at me. "I plan to come back to the States by the time Mari gets close to her due date. We'll figure it out. I'll be there no matter what."

Checking his phone, he takes a generous sip of his coffee before standing.

"I hate to cut out of here already, but I've got a flight out of Omaha back to New York in a few hours, then I'm catching a red-eye back to Hong Kong." Alec places his phone back in his pocket.

My father rises before walking closer and extending a hand. "This situation may not be ideal, Alec, but I appreciate you stepping up to do the right thing."

Alec gives him a tight-lipped nod. "Of course. Was a bit of a shock to me, but a good friend kind of put things into perspective for me, and I knew I couldn't leave Mari like that."

"I'll show you out." I get up from the table, heading toward the front door as my mom wraps Alec in a warm hug.

Once we're outside, he climbs into his car, and I stand outside the driver's window.

"Thanks again," I say.

We spent all day together, trying to figure out the logistics of this entire thing. He says if I wanted to move back to the city, he'd ensure I had a comfortable apartment and that our child would attend the best schools. But with as much as Alec travels, I think I should stay here and raise the baby in Nebraska, where my family can help. He vowed to help me either way.

He also vowed to spend as much time with the baby as possible when he's stateside.

I hope he wasn't just telling me what I wanted to hear, but for now, I have every reason to believe he meant what he said.

"Hey, Alec ..." I lean into his window. I hate that I'm about to ask this, but I have to know. "What did Hudson say to you that made you change your mind?"

He leans back in his seat, staring straight ahead at my parents' garage door and the old basketball hoop attached at the top.

He exhales. "It was more in the delivery than the actual message."

"What do you mean?"

"I've known Hudson my entire life, and when I told him about how I didn't want to be a father and how I wanted you to get rid of it, I'd never seen him so angry. He told me to do the right thing," he says. "And there was this fire in his eyes like I've never seen. He said I only had one chance to do the right thing. Those words really resonated with me after that. This baby's coming into the world, and it's only going to be born once. If I miss that or birthdays or anything else, there's no going back."

"When did he say this to you?"

He turns to me. "A few hours after you left Sea La Vie."

I rise, taken aback.

So this man was furious with me for hiding the pregnancy ... but he still had it in him to make damn sure Alec knew he should do the right thing?

"Hudson loves you, Mari," Alec says, nodding. "I've never seen him care that much about anyone. Not even my sister." He starts his engine. "Anyway, I hope you guys can work things out. It'd be a shame if you couldn't. You guys seemed really happy back in Montauk. Like, genuinely happy."

Stepping away from the car, I give him a wave and watch as he pulls out of the drive.

Heading back in, I slip on my sneakers and tell my parents I'm taking a walk. It's dusk now, the sun just dipping under the horizon, and in the distance, the lights are on at the Frank Lloyd Wright house.

I don't know what I'm going to say when I get there, but something is compelling me, pulling me in that direction.

Seeing Hudson so jealous at the coffee shop earlier and hearing how he defended me when he didn't have to ... it changes things.

I wanted to be done with him.

I wanted to cut my losses and move on.

But I don't think I could if I tried. And god have I tried.

Five minutes later, I'm a couple of houses down from his, my heart racing a thousand beats per second.

There's a white Mercedes in his driveway, and upon closer inspection, I spot two shadows in the front window by the door. They're standing close together, nodding and probably chatting. It's a woman, her hourglass curves exceedingly obvious by the shadow her body makes against the glass.

She reaches for his shoulder, then his face. Touching him. Standing closer, closer still.

A moment later, the door opens and a gorgeous platinum blonde bombshell steps out, giving him a tiny wave with her fingertips before her cherry lips spread into a sex kitten smirk. I watch as she brushes her hair from her face, wearing the smile of a woman who's stumbled across a man who makes her feel alive again.

I know that smile.

I know that feeling.

Hudson stands in the doorway, watching her leave, and she struts down the concrete steps and paved sidewalk to her waiting car, her hips swinging with each step. Once she's gone, he disappears inside.

Hours ago he was flying into a jealous rage at the sight of me having coffee with Alec, but it seems as though he wasted no time finding a pretty little thing to ease his pain.

The vision of him watching her walk away is what kills me.

And here I thought Hudson had changed.

This was a bad idea, and for that reason, I'm going home.

Chapter Forty-two

Hudson

Alexa Lowell's headlights flick on, lighting up the living room of the house as I shut the front door. A stack of listings rest on a nearby saw horse. She stopped by tonight because she found a whole bevy of Orchard Hill homes all in desperate need or renovating.

When I told her I wasn't interested, that the FLW home was a one-and-done type of venture for me, she seemed discouraged but not dissuaded.

I walked her to the door, but she lingered, telling me all about Orchard Hill and how there's this little restaurant made out of an old train depot south of the square that she'd love to take me to sometime.

Her treat.

She then proceeded to brush lint off my shoulder—any excuse she could find to touch me.

This woman had no finesse. She may have

been beautiful, but she was as clear as cellophane.

And most importantly, she's not Mari.

When Alexa finally left, I stood on the front steps, watching her navigate the jagged, broken concrete in those sky high fuck-me heels she wore to my construction zone. I know an opportunist when I see one, and the last thing I need is some small-town real estate agent breaking her neck on my sidewalk. A woman like that would waste no time calling her attorney on speed dial and ensuring the lawsuit is filed the very next day.

Locking the front door, I exhale. This place is coming along nicely. Electricians and plumbers will be working around the clock the next few days and the dry wall crew and roofers should be here early next week. After that, I'll focus on the interior finishes, keeping everything in line with the original FLW design elements, and with any luck, this thing will be restored to her original glory and I'll be on my way.

I thought about keeping this house, but that would be pointless.

I have no business being here in Orchard Hill.

Mari made it perfectly clear she doesn't

want to be with me.

She's moving on.

And I should do the same.

Chapter Forty-three

Mari

There's something soothing about the feel of cool dirt between my fingers. Before plucking a small white petunia from its container, I dig a small hole with my hand trowel. Mom sprained her wrist last night at bowling but Dad had already purchased a hundred dollars' worth of petunias, impatiens, hostas, and marigolds, so I told her I'd handle it.

It's win-win anyway.

There's only so much Wheel of Fortune watching and coffee shop shifts I can distract myself with before my mind circles back to the inevitable.

Him.

"Mari."

Dusting the dirt from my hands, I turn toward the familiar voice, quelling the simultaneous swell of butterflies and swirl of tension in my stomach.

"Hudson," I say, pushing myself up from the grassy patch of yard beneath the old maple tree I used to climb as a child.

He's dressed for a jog and judging by the thin sheen of sweat gracing his muscled upper body, I'm not the first stop on his route.

"Just came by to tell you my accountant is making a deposit on Monday," he says, hands hooked on his hips. My eyes fall to the muscled V pointing toward his shorts before meeting his gaze.

"For what?"

"It's a pro-rated amount," he says. "I'm paying you for the month of work you did."

"I thought the contract said if I didn't finish the agreement in full, I wouldn't be paid at all?"

"It does say that," he says. "But I didn't feel it was a fair deal for you, Mari. I just want to do the right thing."

"It's not necessary." I stand up straight. "I don't need a handout."

"I employed you," he says, his voice holding that chilled quality I once knew so well. Only Hudson could be so cold and so generous at the same time. "You should be compensated."

We stand in quietude, or maybe it's an emotional impasse.

I half expect him to offer one last apology before he goes, one final try to get something out of me. But he says nothing, he simply studies my face before eyeing the distance toward his house.

"Goodbye, Mari." He heads back to the sidewalk, but I'd feel remiss if I didn't tell him that I think about him all the time, even when I don't want to.

"I have this rubber band," I say, calling after him.

He stops, his hands on his hips as he turns to me with twisted brows.

"I wear it on my wrist sometimes, and every time I think of you, I snap it," I say, giving an earnest chuckle. "I thought I could condition myself not to think about you as much, but all it does is leave welts and the second they're gone, you're back in my mind again."

I expect him to come closer to me, but he stays, feet planted on the chipped sidewalk. It hurts more than I thought it would, feeling the sting of emotional and physical distance as it lingers between us.

347

"The worst is when I'm lying in bed at night," I say, "tossing and turning and thinking about you. About us. I play all these scenarios in my head, asking 'what if, what if, what if.' And then knowing you're right up the street?"

I shake my head.

"I hate it. I hate that I want you. I hate that I want to be with you when all you've done so far is hurt me and prove that you're probably going to hurt me again," I say, feeling the sting of tears rim my eyes. "But I thought you should know. I'm guessing I'm not going to see you again after this, and I wanted to say it when I had the chance."

He's quiet, watching me with an unmoving stance.

"You left a mark on me." I place my hand over my heart. "Good or bad, it's there. And it's going to be there forever. And I don't quite know what to do with that yet, but I guess I'll figure it out one of these days."

Hudson lifts his hand to his face, rubbing his eyes before pinching the bridge of his nose and breathing out.

A weight anchors my chest as a rush of emotions flood to my surface. A cry builds. I blink away a single tear because I refuse to cry in front of him.

"I liked you a lot," he says, breaking his silence.

His use of past tense breaks my heart, but I'm not sure what I expected. He came back for me, and I let him go. Many, many times. A candle doesn't reignite after you've blown it out.

Hudson takes elongated strides toward me, his lips flat as his face grows somber. I brace myself for the worst, for the conversation I knew would need to happen sooner or later.

We did this to ourselves. We were careless, frivolous with our emotions. Too generous with our hearts when we had no business doing so. It's no wonder we wound up in a free-fall, spiraling back down to the earth only to crash and burn.

You can't come back from that.

"But then I realized it was turning into something more," he says. "That last night we spent together, Mari, something changed. I realized I was falling in love with you. I didn't want to believe it at first because it was happening so fast. I didn't think it was possible actually." He glances away, pausing. "But the next day, when you came to me with your news, I'd never felt so upset because I knew this was going to change things. Not only did you lie to me in a roundabout way, but knowing you had a piece of Alec inside you, a connection with him that you were never going to have with me … that's what hurt the most. And that's when I knew. That's when I knew I was falling in love with you." He pulls in a deep breath. "I love you, Mari."

The weight of his words sink into every part of me before settling in my chest.

But it still hurts.

"You should know that telling you was the hardest thing I've ever done in my entire life," I say. "I didn't want to hurt you." Clearing my throat, I add, "But imagine how I felt when your mother tells me you were never expected to marry Audrina. You lied to me, Hudson. I agreed to help you. But I didn't agree to be used for some sick little revenge fantasy."

His eyes squint, and he bites his lower lip before lowering his head.

"Yeah," he says, exhaling before pinching the bridge of his nose. "She was my first love. We were together for years, planning to marry. I found out she was fucking my best friend, and I guess it kind of did a number on me. I'm over her now, of course. Have been for years. But I couldn't suppress this part of me that wanted to get one last dig at her. When we were kids, we always said that if neither of us were married by thirty, we'd marry each other. This would've been the year. Guess I wanted to stick it to her one last time, and watching her see me happy, knowing she could see that I'd moved on and found someone a million times better than her, was the final piece that I needed to close that chapter. In retrospect, it was really fucking sideways thinking, and I'm sorry I pulled you into it."

My arms fold across my chest and I pull in a deep breath. As much as I want to be angry with him still, I can't.

"That explains so much about you," I say. "That explains *everything* about you, actually."

"What do you mean?"

"You were heartbroken. You couldn't trust anyone after what she did, so you became cold and unfeeling. You refused to commit to another woman because you were scared of getting hurt again," I say. "And the fact that you needed to do something so extreme in order to feel vindicated once and for all, as fucked up as it is, Hudson, is actually understandable. You're only human. And you were hurting."

He rolls his eyes, sniffing. "There's no excuse for what I did. Don't feel sorry for me, Mari."

"I don't," I say. "But I get it."

Inhaling the scent of flowers and soil and feeling the lawn heat beneath my bare feet and the morning sun, I give him a surrendering gaze.

"So what now?" I ask. "Where do we go from here?"

His brows lift, as if he's shocked that I'm alluding to the fact that maybe this isn't over for me.

"You still want to be with me?" he asks.

Biting my lip and holding out my red, rubber-snapped wrist, I say, "Yeah, Hudson. For some completely insane reason ... I do."

He reaches for me, cradling my hips in his hands and pulling me against his sweaty, iron-steel physique, and I laugh.

"It feels good to hold you again." His blue gaze captures mine, and he brushes my hair from my eyes. "God, I've missed you."

"Before we get things back on track, I have to ask you one thing," I say.

"Anything."

"At the risk of sounding like a jealous psycho girlfriend, who was that blonde girl leaving your house last night?" I ask, one eye squinted.

His full lips smirk. "You were stalking me?"

"Just answer the damn question, Rutherford."

"That was my real estate agent. She came by to drop off some listings she wanted me to consider."

"I have to admit, watching you stare at her as she left made me a little … jealous. And I'm not the jealous type."

Dragging his hand across his mouth he chuckles. "She was in six-inch heels. And that sidewalk is a broken fucking mess. I was just ensuring I wasn't about to have a lawsuit on my hands."

Oh.

"Fair enough," I say. "One more thing though."

"What now?" He stifles a chuckle, and I love the relief in his eyes. It gives me hope.

"No more secrets. No more lies," I say. "Ever again. No matter what."

"Deal."

"And another thing," I add.

"You're not holding back with the contingencies, are you?"

"I want us to apologize to my parents. And yours," I say. "Together."

"Fair enough."

"One last thing." I lift on my toes, placing my hands on his shoulders and grinning. My body is ripe with anticipation, hungry with want.

"Okay …"

"Kiss me like you did the first time," I say.

Hudson wastes no time, his mouth finding mine, claiming me as his while his hand slides along my jaw and the other circles my waist. I'm not sure if my feet are touching the ground or the butterflies in my stomach have any intentions of slowing down. All I know is he's ruined me for any other man.

And now … after everything … I'm finally okay with that.

Chapter Forty-four

Hudson

Mari stepping through the FLW house that night feels nothing short of surreal at this point, but after everything that's transpired, I'm glad she's here.

"Wright was known for horizontal lines and wide open floor plans," I say. "Everything is supposed to feel organic, and as you're standing outside, the house is meant to blend in with the flat, Midwestern prairie. There's this sense of unity with his homes. Everything works together. Everything fits. It's all very natural and a lot of people feel that this type of harmonious design—"

"—it's beautiful," she says, gushing as she moves from space to space, room to room. "I always thought this house looked so dark from the outside, but it's not at all. There are so many windows."

"The linear frames on the top half of the walls let in more light than you'd think." I follow her. "Oh. Before I forget, I have to go back to the city tomorrow. I'll be here every other week and any other time you need me. Why don't you come with? We can go back and forth together."

"That's a lot of traveling." She glances down, her hand on her stomach. "Maybe sometimes?"

"Why don't you just move back with me?" I propose a greedy solution without so much as thinking it over, but it doesn't matter. I want to be with this woman, and I'll move heaven and earth.

Mari locks eyes with me, sucking her lower lip. "I don't want to raise the baby in the city."

"And why not?"

"I love the city." She spreads her hand over her chest. "New York is everything. But it's a different way of life, and I want this baby to grow up close to family, in a cozy little town that lives life a little slower. I don't want to shuffle this kid up and down Manhattan from preschool interview to preschool interview and then wonder how the hell I'm going to afford rent and tuition."

"Mari, it wouldn't be like that," I say, head tilted. "I'd take care of you. Both of you."

"It's kind of you to offer, but my mind is

357

made up. I'm staying here." Her eyes hold a mix of both sadness and hope. "I hope that doesn't change anything ... between us."

Pulling her against me, I press my lips to the top of her head. "Never."

Cupping her face, I lift her chin until her lips align with mine, then I taste their sweetness.

"In that case, there's one room I wanted to show you." I say.

Taking her hand in mine, I lead her past the kitchen and through the reading room, down a hallway and around a corner until we find a cozy bedroom on the east side of the house next to the master suite.

"Might be hard to imagine it now, but I thought this could be your nursery." I look to Mari, waiting for her reaction and watching as disbelief registers on her face. "These windows are high enough so daylight will start to peek through just after sunrise in the morning. The sun sets in the west, so the room should be nice and dark in the evening. I don't know much about babies or how they sleep, but I assume those things might help when you're trying to establish some kind of bedtime routine."

"Hudson ..."

"The room's big enough for a crib and a rocking chair," I say, moving about. "You could put a changing table here. The closet is good-sized too. And you're just a few steps away from the master."

"I can't live here," she says, fighting a smile that tells me she'd do it in a heartbeat.

"I want you to," I say. "I thought about selling it. And then I thought about donating it to some local historical society. But I decided earlier today that I want you to have it."

"That's too generous. I can't. I'd love to. But I can't."

"Why not?" I scoff.

"You can't just give me a house," she says. "That's insane."

"It's my gift to you," I say. "Besides, you can't live with your parents the rest of your life. You need a place to call your own—you and the baby. This house is perfect for a family. There's a huge yard out back and a huge oak tree just waiting for a custom fort—which I'd be happy to design. Plus, you love this street. And you can't put a price on history."

"You don't have to sell me on this house," she says. "I know it's going to be incredible by the time you're finished. But you can't just give it to me."

"I can. And I am."

She saunters up to me, playfully slapping my chest before rising on her toes and pressing her sweet mouth against mine.

"I don't even know what to say right now." Her eyes are lit from within, and she can't stop grinning. "You'll live here, too, right?"

"Do you want me to?"

Mari nods quickly, lips pulling wide as she slips her arms over my shoulders and rises on the balls of her feet.

Sliding my hands down her outer thighs, I pull her up and against me, carrying her to the next room where I've been sleeping when I'm here. There's a queen-sized air mattress on the floor and canvas painter's cloths covering the windows. A small lamp in the corner gives off just enough light, but I'm not concerned about the ambience or amenities right now.

Mari slides down my body, her fingers tugging at her clothes then mine before she falls to her knees and takes me in her mouth. Her free hand travels up my lower stomach, then higher, her nails digging into my flesh as she swirls her tongue around the tip of my aching cock, tasting the bead of precum as it forms.

Taking her time, she indulges me as if the pleasure's all hers, but my impatience gets the better of me, and the craving of her taste on my tongue forces me to interrupt.

"Lie on the mattress," I tell her, dropping to my knees and pumping my cock in my hands. The mere sight of this woman gets me hard as a fucking rock.

Mari lies back, and my fingers skim the soft flesh between her knees, rising higher until I reach the apex. Sliding a finger between her slick folds, I lower my mouth to her glistening pussy to taste her arousal.

Soft moans leave her lips as I slip my tongue between her seam and circle her tender clit. Sliding my left hand up her soft belly toward her swollen breasts, I feel her quiver as I help myself to a handful.

Her body, her heart ... it all belongs to me now.

And mine to her.

Rising over her fevered body, my eyes catch the wanton gaze in hers, and I position the tip of my cock at her wet pussy, pushing myself inside her with one fell thrust.

Mari lifts her arms above her head, sighing and wrapping her legs around my sides. Her hips rock as I thrust, settling into the perfect rhythm.

Slowing down, I take my time so we can both enjoy this. Too many times over the years, I've taken my greedy fill and shown the woman the door the second it was over, biding my time until my next lay. I always needed to be the one to say goodbye, the one to cut the ties first. It was an assembly line void of emotion, with just enough satisfaction to meet my feral needs.

But it's different now.

I want this to last.

And I want it to last forever.

"I love you, Mari," I whisper, our eyes meeting. I said it to her outside her house earlier, but she never said it back. Granted, we were both a bit worked up, but I think she needs to hear it again. And I want to tell her. I want to tell her how special she is to me. "You're the second woman I've ever said that to, but this is the first time I've ever meant it. And I know that because you've shown me what it means to look into the eyes of a woman who doesn't want anything from me but … me."

With a slow, gentle smile, she cups my face in her hands. "I love you too."

She loves me.

Maribel Collins … loves me.

Chapter Forty-five

Mari

"Oh, shit." I wake to the sensation of warm sun on my face as it bakes through the painter's cloths covering the prairie-style windows of the master bedroom.

"What?" Hudson stirs awake, rolling to his side and throwing his arm over me.

"I forgot to tell my parents I wasn't coming home last night."

He chuckles. "What are you? Seventeen?"

Scrambling up from the mattress, I gather my clothes from the floor, tugging them on and yanking them into place as I fluff my hair.

"They worry," I say. "I'm the only kid they've got, so ..."

"Yeah," he says, sitting up. "Not that I can relate, but I get it."

"I'm going to have to explain this, you know. I've been cursing your name for weeks," I say. "Anyway, care to join me? Maybe we can get that little apology thing out of the way while we're at it?"

I toss him a wink. He's not getting out of this.

Smirking, he sits up, rubbing his eyes. The blanket rests at his waist and I enjoy the view of his tan, muscled arms and shoulders as I replay last night in my mind.

"Just let me grab a shower," he says, "then we'll go."

Twenty minutes later, we stroll hand-in-hand down the block and around the corner. My parents are generally forgiving people, but this situation might very well be the exception ... we won't find out until we get there.

I open the front door a few minutes later, glancing up the split foyer toward the kitchen table where my mother rises as if I've startled her.

"Abel, she's home," she calls.

My father's slow yet thunderous footsteps trail from the upstairs hallway and I brace myself, squeezing Hudson's hand tight.

"I'm sorry," I say to them, searching their faces for any indication of how this is going to go.

I'm prepared for a lecture. If my pregnant daughter—grown adult or not—went for a walk and failed to return home without so much as a call, I'd let her have it.

"Next time, call." Mom sighs, heading to the kitchen sink and rinsing some plates before starting a load of dishes in the dishwasher.

Hudson and I exchange looks before climbing the stairs to the main level and taking a seat at the kitchen island.

"I hope I didn't keep you up all night," I say. "You were probably worried."

"We knew where you were," my dad says.

"You did?" I half-laugh.

"Where else would you be?" Mom tsk-tsks. "All you talk about is Hudson, Hudson, Hudson. We knew he was in town. You went for a walk; we saw you head that way. We figured it out."

"You have to give us more credit than that," Dad adds.

Sitting up straight, I glance at Hudson again.

He shrugs.

"We had a serious talk last night," Hudson begins, turning toward my father. "We've each apologized for the hurt we caused one another. And we've realized we want to make this work. We're *going* to make this work."

He turns to my mother.

"I love your daughter," he says. "And I'm sorry for what I put you through—for misleading you. I promise I'll never hurt her again. She's got me—all of me—for the rest of her days."

My parents are quiet for a moment, letting his words sink in, and then my mom comes around the island, throwing her arms around his shoulders.

"Welcome back," she says, her tone warm and her smile gracious.

My father approaches Hudson like a quiet storm, apprehensive at first and then aggressively coming in for a handshake.

"You get one more chance," he says. "Don't blow it."

Hudson meets his hand and they lock eyes. "I won't, sir."

Chapter Forty-six

Mari

Three weeks later …

I didn't think I'd be showing this soon, but I swear there's a bump there.

Or maybe it's last night's five course dinner at Tavern on the Green …

Rolling over in Hudson's bed, I'm greeted with an early morning Manhattan skyline and a reminder of how much I've missed it these last several weeks.

I came back with him this week because with everything going on, I forgot to transfer my medical records from Dr. Gupta's office to one in Orchard Hill, and since I already had my twelve-week ultrasound scheduled, it was easier just to come here.

"Your appointment's in an hour." Hudson

takes a seat on the edge of his bed, a plush gray towel wrapped around his narrow waist and a blue toothbrush sticking out of his perfect mouth. The scent of aftershave and clean soap permeates the air, and I close my eyes, dragging it into my lungs. I wish I could bottle up this moment, keeping it on standby every time I miss him.

I'll be flying home solo this week while he stays and gets caught up at the office. He's bringing on a partner soon, on a temporary basis, to lighten the load as he finishes the Frank Lloyd Wright house, but I have a feeling the further along the pregnancy goes, the more he'll want to spend his time in the Midwest.

Tossing the covers off my legs, I climb out of bed and shuffle to his bathroom.

"You should've woke me up this morning," I call out. "We could've saved water."

He chuckles. "I couldn't wake you. You looked so peaceful. And you needed the rest."

Peeling my clothes off, I start the shower. From the corner of my eye, I catch Hudson stealing a peek through the cracked door. But is it really stealing if it belongs to you in the first place?

"Give me a half hour," I call, stepping into

the marble tiled shower and letting the water drip down my body in jet-streamed rivulets.

Closing my eyes, I softly hum Bob Marley's *Three Little Birds* because for the first time in months, I know that every little thing is going to be all right.

***

"Maribel Collins?" A young nurse in baby pink scrubs calls my name from a doorway, and Hudson and I follow her down a long hallway. "How are you feeling?"

"Great," I say.

"Wonderful." She turns to smile as we walk, and then she veers a corner, stopping at a darkened room with an ultrasound machine and a low bed in the corner. "Well, we're going to start with the sonogram first and get some measurements, and then Dr. Gupta will be in to talk to you and answer any questions that you or your husband might have."

"He's not my husband," I say. Not sure why I felt the need to point that out, but I did. And it's done.

"Not yet," Hudson adds, winking.

The nurse smiles, like we're adorable, and then she tells me to lie back on the table and the technician will be in shortly to get started.

"You going to call Alec?" I ask.

"Already on it." Hudson holds up his phone where Alec is FaceTime'd in from Hong Kong. It must be almost midnight.

Alec's been great the last few weeks. He checks on me and the baby almost every day via text, and we've been talking on the phone at least once a week. He's really making an effort, and he's more involved than I thought he would be. For that I'm exceedingly relieved.

When the sonographer steps in, she dims the lights and quickly does a double take when she spots Hudson holding his phone up. For a moment, I contemplate explaining my situation to her, but I bite my tongue. It's none of her business, and I don't have to justify this arrangement to anyone.

It's absolutely perfect just the way it is.

Funny how, just months ago, I thought I'd be doing this all by myself.

And now I have Hudson and Alec and a baby who's going to grow up surrounded with love and support.

I lift the hem of my shirt and the sonographer squirts a warm jelly-like substance across my lower belly before pressing the transducer against my skin. She moves it back and forth, distributing the gel and concentrating on the grainy black and white image on the screen.

"There we go," she announces a moment later.

The three of us have locked eyes on the tiny monitor, waiting to see something that resembles anything other than a white blob.

She drags her mouse across the image, taking measurements alongside with the random, "That's good. Looking good. That's normal."

I glance at Hudson, and he smiles, and though it's dark in the room, I can almost swear he's got a tear in his eye.

"We're going to listen to the baby's heart," she says.

I close my eyes and hold my breath as the rapid, steady thump and whoosh fills the small room. It's the best sound I've ever heard in my entire life.

"Everything looks great," she says. "Dr. Gupta will be in shortly."

She hands me a warm cloth to clean my belly before flicking the lights on and leaving us alone. We say goodbye to Alec, telling him we'll keep him posted, and he sends us off with a late night yawn from the other side of the globe.

"That was ..." Hudson's voice trails off. "Wow. Kind of makes it all real."

I nod. "I thought that last time, but I was too in shock to really enjoy it then. This was incredible. Thank you so much for coming with me today."

"Of course," he says. "I wouldn't miss it. Let me know when all of your appointments are and I'll be there."

"You going to the office after this?" I ask.

"Thought I'd take the day. Spend it with you."

"Wait a minute, do I know you?" I tease. "The entire time I worked for you, you didn't take a single day off."

"I'm taking you for lunch, maybe do some

shopping for the baby," he says. "And then my parents are coming over tonight. They want to see you."

"They want to see me?" I point at myself, like he could possibly be speaking to anyone else.

"Yeah," he says. "I told them we're back together, and they wanted to see you immediately."

"Should I be worried that they're specifically coming to the city just to see me?" Every time I look back at the moment I left Sea La Vie, I cringe. I was so caught up in the moment, in the emotions, I let it get the best of me. I can't help but think I could've handled things with a little more tact and dignity, but I never thought I'd be seeing any of those people again.

"We'll find out." He chuckles, and I take solace in the fact that he's clearly not worried.

***

"Mr. Rutherford, your parents are here." Marta stands in the doorway of Hudson's bedroom, her eyes moving from him to me and back. Ever since I came back, she's been warming up to me.

Hudson says she didn't want to get attached before and it was nothing personal.

"We'll be out shortly." He turns to me. "Why do you look so nervous?"

"I don't know?" I bite my lip. I've been rehearsing everything I want to say to them all day, namely my humble apology, but not knowing why they needed to immediately see me makes this meeting that much more nerve wracking.

He takes my hand, leading me down the hallway toward his living room where Conrad and Helena are seated on the Chesterfield sofa.

I lock eyes with his mother first, and she stands.

His father clears his throat, tugging at his navy sport coat.

"How are you feeling, Maribel?" Helena asks, her voice as gentle as a cloud.

"Great," I say. "Just had an appointment earlier today. Baby's healthy."

"That's wonderful," she says, motioning toward the seat beside her. "Why don't you have a seat, dear?"

I pad across the room, taking the spot beside her and noticing a little blue Tiffany's bag nestled beneath the coffee table.

"I wanted you to know," she begins, "that we accept you—and your baby—into our family with open arms."

My eyes well, my chest tingles with fullness.

"We've shared many things with the Sheffields in our time," Conrad says. "Why not share a grandchild?"

"We think it'll be a wonderful thing," she says, reaching for my hand and taking it between her palms. "We adore you, Maribel."

"Really?" My voice breaks.

"Why do you seem so shocked?" Helena laughs, glancing at Conrad.

"From the moment I met you, I knew you were a good girl," Conrad says. "And we knew that our boy was crazy about you. All a parent can ever really hope for is that their child finds love and happiness, and Hudson found that with you."

"I'm so sorry for lying to you both," I say.

"Yes," Hudson says. "We want to make it clear, we accept full responsibility for our actions, and we're deeply remorseful."

"Thank you," Helena says. "We appreciate that."

"Thank you for accepting … us." I place my hand on my stomach.

"Of course," Conrad says.

"We brought you something." Helena reaches for the blue Tiffany bag, handing it over. "I'm hoping the baby doesn't already have one of these."

I smile, silently assuring her the baby does not, in fact, have a single thing from Tiffany & Co.

Digging past white tissue paper, I pull out a small box containing a silver rattle.

"Thank you," I say, gently wrapping my arms around her. "I love it."

"Just a small keepsake," she says as I pull away. "Hudson had one. A gift from my mother-in-law. You'll get to meet her next month at my niece's wedding in Portland. You'll be joining us, won't you? As Hudson's plus one?"

I glance at Hudson, vaguely recalling when we'd signed the original agreement and he mentioned that I'd be accompanying him to a slew of weddings and family gatherings over the course of the summer. But that was then. And he's yet to ask me as his date ... officially.

"Will you join me as my plus one for cousin Jennifer's wedding next month?" he asks, practically reading my mind.

"I'd love to," I say.

"Wonderful." Helena claps her hands together before standing. "We won't keep you. We just wanted to stop by and give you your gift and welcome you back to the family with open arms."

"Thank you." I follow them to the door with Hudson behind me, his hand on the small of my back. "We'll see you next month!"

She blows a kiss on the tips of her fingers before waving goodbye to us and disappearing into the hallway behind Conrad.

The second they're gone, I exhale.

"That wasn't so bad, was it?" Hudson says, drawing me in.

I place my hands on his chest, staring up

379

into his deep blues. I'd live in them if I could, I love them so.

"So what now?" I ask.

His lips curl into a devilish grin and his hands slide down my sides, lifting me and carrying me back to his room.

Burying my face in his neck, I throw my arms around his corded-steel shoulders and breathe him in.

I love him.

So hard.

Epilogue

Hudson

Six months later…

Mari cradles Grey Hudson Sheffield in her arms. All seven pounds and eight ounces of him are swaddled in a white muslin blanket covered in baby giraffes, and he's fast asleep, out cold with a full belly. She wears exhaustion like a rock star, exuberant and glowing despite a twenty-two-hour labor and two hours of pushing.

Sitting beside her, I can't take my eyes off these two beautiful, tired souls.

"I can't stop looking at him," she says, her voice a gentle breeze. "Isn't he perfect?"

"Yeah." I place my hand over hers. "He really is."

Alec is seated on the other side of the hospital bed, watching his newborn son sleep. He flew to Nebraska from Hong Kong a couple of weeks ago in anticipation of the birth, but Mari ended up going a week past her due date.

The three of us spent a lot of time catching up, talking about our hopes and dreams for the little guy.

I have to hand it to Alec. He completely proved me wrong about him. He's really handling this situation better than I thought he would, and he's going to start taking fewer international jobs so he can be around more.

Mari's eyes flutter. She's struggling to stay awake.

My phone lights up with a text from Mari's friend Isabelle asking how everyone's doing before letting us know she's going back to bed. She FaceTime'd in for the birth, and she plans to visit as soon as the fanfare dies down and Mari is up for a house guest.

"We should let you both rest," I say, scooping Grey from her arms and placing him in the bassinette.

Mari doesn't fight it, she simply nods and lets her cheek fall to the pillow.

Alec and I sneak out of the room, heading

toward the hospital cafeteria. We're both in dire need of a good night's rest, but neither of us want to leave those two just yet.

"Hey, man," Alec says, stopping me halfway down the hall.

"Yeah?"

"Thank you," he says, eyes earnest. "Thank you for taking care of them these last several months when I was gone. And thank you for accepting Grey the way you have. I can only hope to be half the man you are someday."

"Give yourself more credit." I lift my hand to his back, squeezing his shoulders. "You've done well. And we're in this together. For life."

"One big, happy family." Alec chuckles and we turn the corner.

"The way it's always been."

***

Lying awake, I stare at the ceiling. Grey's been home two weeks now, and his sleeping schedule is still pretty erratic. Alec left for a new gig in San Francisco yesterday, and Mari and I are still working out some kind of nighttime schedule that works for us both.

Living in Orchard Hill full time now has been quite the adjustment. Some nights it's too quiet and isolated. Other nights it's pure bliss and peaceful.

Grey's tiny cry plays over the intercom and Mari instantly shuffles awake, scrambling to get out of bed.

Placing my arm across her, I say, "I'll get it this time."

"You sure?" she mutters, half asleep.

"Yeah. Go back to sleep." Climbing out of bed, I trek into the nursery next door, scooping him out of his crib and lying him on the changing table. He's wet. And probably hungry.

A small envelope rests at the center of the changing pad, with my name scribbled across it in Mari's handwriting. Tucking it in the waistband of my sweats, I change little Grey before carrying him to the kitchen to fix a bottle.

Several minutes later, we're situated in the rocking chair in the living room, a small Tiffany lamp splashing gentle stained glass colors on the wall behind us.

Pulling out the letter, I unfold the linen paper and give it a read.

Dear Mr. Rutherford,

I humbly request that you accept this as my pledge to love you now and forever, until the end of time. I have no intentions of ever stepping down from my position as the woman who's insanely and hopelessly wild about you. I'll do my best to ensure this is a smooth transition for our relationship, but I cannot promise to exercise self-restraint at all times in your presence because, truth be told, I find it impossible to keep my hands off you most of the time.

With fondness and gratitude,

Maribel Collins

"Your mother is cute, Grey," I whisper, chuckling to myself as he downs his bottle in record time. I rock him for a moment, watching his eyes fuse shut as he settles into another several hours of sleep.

Having a newborn is sweet, delirious exhaustion, and I wouldn't change it for the world.

I trace my fingers down his perfect nose. Grey is the spitting image of Mari so far, and I don't see a lot of Alec in there—at least not yet.

After a few moments and when I'm positive he's down for the count, I rise slowly and carry him back to his crib.

Climbing back into bed with Mari a minute later, I find another envelope on my pillow. With help from the moonlight spilling in from the window above the bed, I quietly slide the letter out and begin to read it.

Hudson,

I will.

Mari

Mari rolls toward me, her full, delicious lips curling into a slow grin as she sits up on her elbow. Her eyes are heavy and her body wants to go back to sleep, but her heart wants me.

And the heart always wins.

"You will?" I lift my brows. A month ago, on a whim, I proposed to her. While she confirmed she was absolutely crazy about me and loved me to the end of the earth and back, she asked for more time. She said there was too much going on at once and she didn't want to get caught up and move too fast.

"Yes, Hudson," she says as I slide under the covers and pull her over top of me, my hands sliding up her sides. "I will marry you."

Ask Me Anything

You asked, I answered!

When did you know you wanted to be a writer? –
Charlene D.

About thirty years ago! I remember being in
preschool and dictating a story to my grandmother
because I didn't know how to write yet. It was
about a frog who had no willpower. But the writing
bug really bit me in first and second grade, during
Writer's Workshop. I still have all my books, too!

Where do your story ideas come from? – Felicia E.

I wish I knew! Every once in a while, I'll be inspired by a weird dream or a little seed of an idea, but most of the time I have no idea where my stories come from. They just kind of show up in my mind, if that makes sense? I thought I was crazy until I read Elizabeth Gilbert's Big Magic, and then I realized I'm not the only one. :-)

Also, you know when you're listening to a song and you kind of escape your thoughts for a while and slip into a daydream? That's kind of how my ideas come to me. I let go of my own thoughts and daydream for a while. Sometimes a bunch of scenes will come to me for a particular book I'm working on, and I'll write them down and piece them together and figure out their order.

Winter Renshaw. Sosie Frost. Two separate people? Confirm or deny. – Sosie F.

Thank you for asking this question, Sosie, because it's time we set the record straight. This may come as a shock to some of you, but Winter Renshaw and Sosie Frost are two *entirely* separate people with approximately 780 miles (and a few years) between them.

How do these characters and their lives come to you? – Ronetta W.

I start with a premise and then conjure up characters who would most be challenged by that premise. The more challenging, the better!

Do you need a best friend? Because I'm available. – Erica W.

The more, the merrier! <3

Who is your favorite author and why? – Carrie S.

Whitney G., hands down! I got hooked on her *Reasonable Doubt* series a few years back, and I'm convinced everything she writes is pure gold. I don't know anyone who can write (and redeem) a sexy alpha jerk like Whitney, and I love, love, love the way her characters banter. The chemistry comes to life in her books.

How old were you when you decided to write your first book? – Libby B.

Aside from crafting stories as a young child, I didn't write my first novel-length book until I was thirty. I started and stopped, started and stopped a bajillion times, never finishing because I was 100% convinced they were never going to be good enough.

How many hours a day do you usually write? –
Denise T.

I aim for three to four when I'm working on a novel. I find anything more than that, my quality suffers and it's not worth it.

If you could get any piece of advice from any other author, what would it be and what would you ask them? – Sandra W.

Mia Asher writes the best sex scenes. I'd love to know if she has any tips! Her writing is so beautiful and poetic and almost rhythmic. It's classy and pretty and chock full of angst and raw emotion. It's no wonder her sex scenes are off the charts amazing.

How much research goes into your books? –

Stephanie P.

It depends! Certain things I've had to research in the past (polygamy and hockey are two that stand out the most for me as I had zero experience with either of those things). Most of the time, I Google as I go, and they're always little random things (the driving distance between two cities, cool hotel names, how to make an Old Fashioned, etc, etc).

Do you have the complete thought of the story before you start or is it more organic? Coming along as you write or a combo of both? - Anthula G.

I used to outline my stories extensively and that helped me to write them really quickly (Never Kiss a Stranger was written in 10 days!). But as I've grown and changed as a writer, I've found myself preferring to make it up as I go. If I know exactly what's going to happen next, I get bored and turned off by the story. So now, I might outline 2-3 chapters at a time and write based on that, and I might know the twists or what's going to happen at the climax or black moment, but getting from one point to another is usually a surprise for me until I'm working on those scenes. I like to let the characters lead the way. The books feel more organic for me that way.

If you had to pick a genre completely out of your comfort zone to write, what would you want to try? – Jessica P.

I don't know about another genre outside of this, but I've always wanted to do a time travel romance! One of these days, maybe I will …

Out of all your books, which character would you want to be? – Kelli J.

Addison from *Never Kiss a Stranger*! I think it would be amazing to live in New York and sell high-end real estate. Maybe it's only glamorous in my mind because I'm sure that's a super stressful, cut-throat career, but that city is pure magic and to be able to step inside of some of those properties would be heaven on earth. Those commissions though … lol.

What genres do you read? How many times do you rewrite a chapter or section of a book to fit a new idea? – Diana S.

I mostly stick to romance and non-fiction (memoirs, parenting books, writing books, that sort of thing). Occasionally I'll grab a bestseller like *Girl on the Train* or *Big Little Lies*.

Have you always wanted to be a writer? – Tereasa J.

For as long as I can remember!

If you could collaborate with any other author, who would you choose? – Mellissa C.

I'd have to say Sosie Frost, because I love her dearly and respect the hell out of her as a writer. We became acquainted a couple years ago in a writer's community when I posted about starting a beta group. Not only has she been a godsend to me professionally because her advice is top notch and she knows her stuff, but we chat online or text every single day and she is the sweetest, smartest, and funniest person ever. Collaborating with her would be a total blast!

Do you have a muse? – Darlene B.

It changes with each book. I try to "cast" my hero and heroine before I start the book so I can put a face and mannerisms on them immediately. If I don't, I tend to change stuff as I go (without realizing it sometimes) and that can be an editing nightmare.

How come Locke only had a novella? – Franci K.

I've received this question quite a bit lately, and while I would have loved to have given Locke a full-length story, I took one look at my schedule for the year and knew it just wouldn't have worked. I have way too much on my plate, so I figured a little bonus novella in the back of *Cold Hearted* was better than nothing. :-)

I seriously don't know how you write and publish so many books in such a short

amount of time. What's your secret to being so prolific? – Sherri M.

It's all about the discipline! I set daily goals for myself (word counts or chapter counts), and I write them down every day. My husband makes fun of me because I'll re-write my to-do list every single day on a fresh sheet of paper, but it's something

I've always done that helps keep me focused on my goals.

How old were you when you published your first book and what inspired you to write it? – Jessica G.

I was thirty-one when I published *Never Kiss a Stranger*, which was my first full-length book. I'd tried my hand at some novellas before that and none of them were doing that well. I always knew I wanted to be a writer and I'd taken several classes in college, but in retrospect, I had no idea what I was doing. I took a step back, obsessively studied my craft, read a bajillion books on writing, listened to about forty RWA seminars, enlisted the help of some amazingly talented author friends, and figured out what I could do to improve my writing. Still to this day, I "study" my negative reviews and read books on the craft of writing. I'm constantly in a state of wanting to get better and better. I'm a bit of a perfectionist, but I don't think that's a bad thing in this industry.

As far as what inspired me to write it, at that time,

everyone was writing "stepbrother romances" and they were all the same for the most part. I wanted to do something trendy but different, so I thought, "What if two people hooked up using a dating app then discovered they were stepsiblings?" And the story was born.

How many books have you written/published to date? — Sabrina G.

Including The Perfect Illusion, I've written 16 novels and 1 novella to date. I have a few more planned for 2017!

Which book was the hardest/most emotional for you to write? Sabrina G.

Definitely Royal. Out of all my books, I think that one had the most amount of emotionally charged scenes. There were some powerful moments and I had to tap into some pretty deep emotions I'd been burying for years. It was cathartic though!

What is your favorite color and favorite flower? –
Sabrina G.

They change with the seasons it seems, but right now my favorite color is geranium red and my favorite flowers are blue hydrangeas!

Want to Ask Me Anything? Send your question to authorwinter@hotmail.com **and I'll include it in my next AMA!**

BOOKS BY WINTER RENSHAW

The Never Series

Never Kiss a Stranger

Never Is a Promise

Never Say Never

Bitter Rivals: a novella

The Arrogant Series

Arrogant Bastard

Arrogant Master

Arrogant Playboy

The Rixton Falls Series

Royal

Bachelor

Filthy

Standalones

Dark Paradise

Vegas Baby

Cold Hearted

ACKNOWLEDGEMENTS

This book would not be possible without the following list of incredibly dear-to-me individuals.

Neda and Liz with Ardent PR – thank you for all of your hard work and understanding.

Louisa, I'm 100% convinced you're the best in the biz. Thank you for your flexibility and understanding and for making the new cover just as beautiful as the original.

Wander and Andrey, thank you for your amazing customer service and behind-the-lens prowess.

Wendy, thank you for your patience and for always being gracious when I miss my deadlines.

K, C, and M, you're my BAEs in this crazy indie author world. I heart you. Thanks for putting up with my MIA-existence these last couple of months.

To my readers and book bloggers, thank you for keeping the lights on at Casa de Renshaw. Your support means the WORLD to me, and I love, love, love you in the truest sense of the word. So much love for you. Thank you for all you do. I'm in this for the long haul, and I hope you are too.

ABOUT THE AUTHOR

Wall Street Journal and #1 Amazon bestselling author Winter Renshaw is a bona fide daydream believer. She lives somewhere in the middle of the USA and can rarely be seen without her trusty Mead notebook and ultra portable laptop. When she's not writing, she's living the American Dream with her husband, three kids, and the laziest puggle this side of the Mississippi.

Like Winter on Facebook.

Join the private mailing list.

Join Winter's Facebook reader group/discussion group/street team, CAMP WINTER.

CPSIA information can be obtained
at www.ICGtesting.com
Printed in the USA
LVOW11s1742230517
535559LV00005B/981/P